———— ★ ————

The John Doe now identified as Dennis Sharp had been shot once in the chest with a .38 caliber handgun at close range. Time of death was estimated at between five and ten hours after the drug bust at the Seaview, although the connection to the Seaview was in my head only. Calculating how long Sharp had been gone, I marveled at how many people had been looking for a dead guy for the last two days.

A hiker had found the body off to the side of a trail in one of Davis's recreation areas, a large stretch of woods known as a good spot for teenagers to go be teenagers. Although the Gulf region has its share of runaways and muggings, an out-and-out murder is quite unusual in my neck of the woods, and the Davis cops had processed the kid pretty quickly. The body had been near an old maintenance shack, and a search of the area had yielded a small backpack with what seemed to be Dennis Sharp's earthly belongings. The backpack's contents had provided few clues regarding Dennis Sharp's final hours, but a crumpled Midnight Taxi Service map in the kid's pocket had suggested he had recently taken a cab ride.

———— ★ ————

REDUCED CIRCUMSTANCES

VINCENT H. O'NEIL

W★RLDWIDE ®

TORONTO • NEW YORK • LONDON
AMSTERDAM • PARIS • SYDNEY • HAMBURG
STOCKHOLM • ATHENS • TOKYO • MILAN
MADRID • WARSAW • BUDAPEST • AUCKLAND

For my brothers and sister

Recycling programs
for this product may
not exist in your area.

REDUCED CIRCUMSTANCES

A Worldwide Mystery/September 2011

First published by St. Martin's Press

ISBN-13: 978-0-373-26766-8

Printed in U.S.A.

Acknowledgments

As always, I am very grateful to my editor, Ruth Cavin, for her expertise and hard work. My thanks also go to Toni Plummer, assistant editor at Thomas Dunne/St. Martin's Minotaur, for always coming up with answers to my sometimes obvious questions. The copy editor for this book, Helen Chin, did a particularly fine job, and I would like to thank her as well. Finally many thanks to Lauren Manzella, Rachel Ekstrom, and all the other folks in the St. Martin's Press publicity department who have worked on the Exile series.

ONE

WE WERE SWABBING OUT the taxis when I first learned about the kid. Cleaning out the cabs was one of the morning rituals for the five drivers of the Midnight Taxi Service, and there was usually at least one interesting tale from the previous night's fares.

"—I mean, I've had people practically throw themselves under the tires before, but this kid sure was in a lather." Billy Lee was the driver doing the talking, his heavy Southern accent always making him sound like he was pulling your leg. Tall, lean, blond-haired and blue-eyed, that morning he was wearing jeans and an aqua blue bowling shirt with "Billy" embroidered in gold lettering on the chest pocket. At first I had thought "Billy Lee" was his first name because all of the other drivers always addressed him that way, but working as night dispatcher gave me access to the drivers' time sheets. Lee was his surname.

"Runnin' from a motel? You never seen that before, Billy Lee? Particularly at this time of year?" This came from Tony Ng, at twenty the youngest driver of the group. Though only one generation removed from Vietnam, Tony was born and raised right there in the Florida

Panhandle and spoke with as pronounced a Southern twang as Billy Lee. It was hard to put that accent together with his dark complexion and the jet-black hair which he parted down the center of his head so that it bobbed when he walked.

"Oh, I'm not sure he was runnin' away from anything, Tony. He was in one heck of a hurry to get somewhere, though, and with all those flashing police lights I wasn't sure if I wasn't going to get hauled in for aidin' and abettin'."

I straightened up when I heard about the police lights. I had been brushing the beach sand out from under the backseat of Tony's cab when Billy Lee had begun his story, but now this was getting interesting. Besides, Tony wasn't making any effort to clean up the front seat of his rig, and I was unwilling to do the whole job, new guy or not.

"Police cars?" I asked as I reached for the Styrofoam cup of coffee sitting on Tony's roof. The Midnight taxis were a collection of different makes, colors, and sizes, and Tony's was a beige four-door which had been bleached almost white by the Panhandle sun. That sun was just making itself visible in the east, starting to shoot rays onto the placid waters of the Gulf across the street from where we were parked.

"Yeah, Frank, and a lot of 'em, too. Musta been half the Davis police force there. You know the motel I'm talkin' about, right? The Seaview?"

"Nebraska's got a better view of the sea," Tony threw

in, leaning back against his vehicle and blowing on his coffee to cool it. The taxi service's owner, Mr. Dominic Corelli, paid for everybody's morning coffee even though he didn't come in until well after nine. He'd stayed on for my first two evenings as night dispatcher before deciding I wasn't going to put him out of business, and the morning coffee run had become one of my duties.

"Now, you don't know that, Tony." Again it was hard to tell if Billy Lee were serious or not. "I'm sure if you climbed up on that flat, droopy roof of theirs you'd have a fine view of the sea."

"What about the cops?" I tried to get them back on track, but the Midnight Service's drivers took great delight in ignoring their new night dispatcher, who was college-educated and a Yankee to boot.

"I bet more than one Seaview guest has gone up there, too." Tony's hair bounced as he nodded to his own words. "I mean, a two-story drop might not kill you, but West Davis is a pretty depressing place and when a man's depressed he'll try anything."

Tony was right about that part. We were parked at a little rest stop in Davis proper, a small grassy area with a couple of picnic tables and a sweeping view of the Gulf of Mexico. Although there was technically no such place as West Davis, the money people who lived in Davis proper and the surrounding area referred to the bad part of town as West Davis whenever they could. I am told they tried to get the place officially labeled that way a few years before, but that a sharp street lawyer from a West Davis strip mall had run circles around them in court, and so the rich folk had been forced to keep the unofficial name going by word of mouth.

Another taxi rolled up and Manny Batista, one of the older drivers, got out. Manny had come to America from Cuba as a teenager with the 1980 Mariel Boatlift, and he liked to tell people that he was one of the inmates Castro had released from Cuba's asylums at the time. He lived two towns over to the east in a small place called Exile. That was where I was currently living and I had gotten to know the police chief quite well, so I had it on good authority that Manny's story was a bit of an exaggeration.

Manny was a short guy, with a barrel chest and arms that looked like they could twist a fire hydrant in half. He wore a pink guayabera, the long Latin shirt, with red roses running down one side. He carefully adjusted the skimmer that never left his head and came over to my car to get his coffee.

Manny's arrival brought Billy Lee and Tony back to the topic of the police; the older man usually had a dampening effect on the younger drivers. Manny had mastered the art of the scornful stare, and seemed to apply it to Billy Lee and Tony more than anyone else. I personally think it was because he regarded the two twenty-somethings as being only one step removed from the college kids they drove around the Panhandle in the spring.

He didn't need The Stare today, though, as he had driven past the Seaview on the way to our little daily rendezvous.

"You should see the circus at the Seaview," he told us. "Newspaper people, television people, cops all over, and even a couple of suits and ties." He concentrated on his coffee, making a face even though I had gotten his preference perfect this time.

"Still?" Billy Lee asked, slightly subdued. He began to take pieces of trash paper from his front seat and drop them in the garbage bag. "They were there last night around eleven, all flashing lights and blasting radios; you'd think they'd be done by now."

Tony had taken an interest in cleaning out his rig, too, so I stayed on break. Maybe Manny would get Billy Lee to keep talking.

"Television camera works better in the daylight," Manny offered as if he were mulling it over instead of pointing out the obvious. "Maybe they waited for sunup to do the formal announcement. You have any idea what it's about?"

Billy Lee came out of the backseat of his cab still holding the garbage bag. "Naw. The place was all lit up as I was driving by, I probably wouldda stopped to look but like I was telling Frank, this kid came running out in front of me and flagged me down."

Manny gave him The Stare.

"Oh, come on, Manny! He might not have even been in the motel at all! Like I said, he ran up to me on the street. He wasn't carrying anything, either, so what was I supposed to do?"

The Cuban kept the gaze fixed on Billy Lee for a moment or two longer before cracking a smile and laughing deep in his chest. "I'm just havin' fun with you, Billy! It's not like we're supposed to grill the fares just because the cops are around."

"Excuse me, sir." Tony had emerged from his taxi and spoke across the vehicle's roof with a deep, authoritative traffic cop's voice. "Have you been involved in any criminal activity this evening? If you have, I may be required to place you under special citizen's arrest— you have the right to remain silent…"

Just then, the final two Midnight drivers rolled up together. They were just returning from a late call for a big party trying to get back to their Panama City hotel.

The Midnight Service had two minivans for occasions like that, and the stories of jamming twice the acceptable number of passengers into those rolling meat lockers were legion. I had been allowed to pilot one of the regular taxis when we were hurting for drivers, but the vans were another thing entirely.

Both vehicles had been dull yellow when I joined the company a month before, but now one was blue. A nasty sideswiping one dark night in a crowded parking lot had made a new paint job pretty much mandatory.

The yellow van made a big turn and ran its two right tires up onto the curb. This was the signal that the van needed to be rinsed out, and I went to get the hose. A spigot stood up out of the ground near the picnic tables, and I began attaching it while Ruby Sears worked his way out of the van.

Ruby was probably fifty years old and the most senior driver. Even Manny did what Ruby told him to do, which was a pretty solid testament to Ruby's common sense and leadership skills. It might also have been recognition of Ruby's enormous size, but I had not yet summoned the nerve to ask. Ruby was probably six feet tall, but he weighed close to three hundred pounds. So there was no way he was going to drive one of the normal rigs.

It would be kind to say that most of Ruby's weight was muscle, but it would not be accurate. Ruby was a big fat black guy who knew more about driving a taxi in the Panhandle than anybody, including Mr. Corelli. Ruby knew all the back routes, all the police, and most of the bouncers at the local clubs. He was also rumored to have chased down two college kids just a year before when they tried to stiff him. He put one in a headlock and sat on the other while dialing his cell phone for the police.

I unwound the green rubber tube until I was standing on the uphill side of the van, and slid the big yellow door back on its runners. Ruby did the same on the other side. (Corelli had searched long and hard for these models, stressing the desirability of shooting water straight through the vehicle.) I began spraying what looked like a ten-course meal off the floor of the van. The hose had one of those pistol grip nozzles that allows the user to get a full spray going instantly and shutting it off just as quickly.

We couldn't, of course, wait until the end of a shift to clean up this kind of mess. Some drivers carried boxes of sawdust, some carried paper shavings, and one even carried kitty litter for the purpose of sopping up this kind of problem until a water point could be reached. Corelli insisted that a liberal dose of disinfectant and some air freshener followed an event like that, and there was always the in-depth cleaning in the morning, when all of the rigs were swabbed out.

Ruby came around to my side of the spray, wearing a light windbreaker despite the heat. A porkpie hat was pushed back on his head, and an inch-long unlit cigar sat in the corner of his mouth. He always looked as if someone had just dragged a set of fingernails across a blackboard, but in the month that I had known him I had found him to be even-minded and generally unexcitable.

"Hoo-wee, Ruby! Was that a bunch of college kids or deep-sea fishermen you were haulin'?" asked Billy Lee, coming over. "Looks like they gutted a Great White right in the back of your rig!"

"From the smell I'd say that red color's mostly wine. But I did pick that gang up at the yacht club—"

"Which one?"

"The Clover. So maybe they were deep-sea fishermen after all." Ruby pointed to a section of the floor that I hadn't hit yet. "Now, am I going to find your rig as clean as this one when I go over there?"

Billy Lee took the hint and moved off while Danny Parsons, the driver of the blue van, crossed the grass and joined us. He was the quiet one in the group, thirty years old like me and also a resident of Exile.

He had once told me that his hair had started receding when he was fifteen, and so he kept the small fringe that was left cut down almost to nothing. He usually wore a baseball cap to protect his scalp from the sun, but this morning the cap was absent. When he handed Ruby a coffee I noticed for the first time that they were the same height although Danny was much leaner. The two were frequently paired off, due to Danny's quiescent nature and the fact that he usually drove the blue van. Danny seemed happiest when he had secured Ruby's approval.

"You know, at this hour of the morning I would not have expected that to happen," Danny observed as I dragged the hose around the other side of the van and began spraying the mess down the storm drain. "When we split them up between us I would not have picked that little guy to be able to do all this."

"Man just had too much fun, is all. Not like we can predict this kind of thing, is it?"

"Now, that would be some trick, wouldn't it, Ruby?"

"Yes, it would, Danny."

And with that slight acknowledgment Danny was good for the day. He ambled off toward the other cabs, taking the communal trash bag from Manny as he went by and beginning to clean out his cab while I began coiling the hose.

"Thank you, Frank," Ruby said. He looked at me strangely, moving his head from side to side as if inspecting a horse he was going to buy. "Frank, have you lost a lotta weight since comin' on board with us?"

Of course he was right, and of course he was the only one who would have noticed. I was wearing a T-shirt that had once hugged a nice little potbelly but now hung on me like laundry drying on the line. I kept the shirt untucked so no one would notice that the cargo pants I was wearing were ready to fall down around my ankles despite two extra notches cut in it.

"Yeah, but this was happening before I came to work with you guys. I was dieting. Looks like I overdid it, huh?"

"Yeah, I do that all the time." He smiled. "Listen, your business is your business, but you sure you're just down here for the sun? I mean, a guy with your education usually isn't hosin' out taxis for a living. You sure there isn't somethin' eatin' you? Maybe somethin' unfinished up north?"

For a moment I wondered if he knew the real truth about my current employment with the Midnight Taxi Service, and my current residence in Exile, Florida, but since I had not confided it to any of the drivers I had to doubt that. I smiled weakly.

"Something like that. Yeah."

SOMETHING LIKE THAT. Yeah. Actually, Ruby had hit it right on the nose and I wasn't at all sure that my weight loss wasn't directly related to my presence in Florida. I had been in the Panhandle for almost a year when I took the job with the Midnight Taxi Service. But the beginning of the trouble went back a good three years.

Then I was the proud owner of a midsize software company which specialized in tailoring applications for our corporate clients. Roughly fifty people worked for me, I was married to a wonderful woman, and everything was great, right up to the point when the whole computer industry went into a nosedive.

Having given much of my early adulthood to building that company, I wasn't about to watch it go down the drain without a fight. So I did two things the Small Business Administration normally tells people not to: First, I put my own money into the business (and watched it disappear in a frighteningly small number of months), and then I went outside the normal banking channels to get more.

None of this was illegal, mind you, but when you go beyond normal lending services you are really taking a chance. These people are sometimes referred to as venture capitalists, and sometimes they are called mezzanine finance, but whatever the name they are usually a group of wealthy people hoping to make some quick money. The best thing that can happen is a speedy recovery, in which case you pay huge interest and get away from the mezzanine folks as fast as possible. The more common result is an ongoing relationship, complete with a mezzanine representative sitting in your office. And sometimes, as in my case, the business continues to decline and the new partners push out the old management.

I fought them on that one, and ended up getting forced into bankruptcy. That was when things really went awry, as a psychotic judge decided to add a new feature to corporate bankruptcy law and attached my future earnings against the settlement of my titanic debts. Normally a bankruptcy settles the debts one way or the other, and the slate is wiped clean, but not so in my case.

My old college roommate, a good friend named Mark Ruben, who was by then a successful corporate lawyer in Manhattan, stepped in at that point and concocted a plan to get the creditors and the judge off my back. My yearly earnings were not subject to confiscation if I stayed below a certain income level, and so Mark had suggested I relocate to a nice, warm part of the country and do part-time work as a fact-checker for local law offices and insurance companies. This kind of work fit my technical background, as much of it involved background checks and court document retrieval, and I picked the Florida Panhandle because many years earlier I had been one of the college kids visiting there on spring break.

Probably threw up in the back of a Midnight taxi, too.

Mark believed that the plan would convince my shadowy creditors to give up on ever getting restitution from me, but I'd been at this for over a year and there was little indication that the message was being received. Mark had called the other night with the unwelcome news that my former partners were interested in getting control of a few software innovations created by my company, the first word from them since the court case had ended. I would have been happy to give up the rotten patents to get my life back, but unfortunately they were sitting in an insurance company's office in Hartford and I currently had no more right to them than the creditors.

At any rate, the fact-checking work had actually proven interesting, and it had brought me into contact with some local private investigators who encouraged me to consider joining their profession. As there is a lot of training and licensing involved in P.I. work, I did not really give this much consideration, but I did help solve a murder that had horsed up one of my insurance investigations along the way. I actually could have benefited financially from that case, but I was still trying to keep the earnings low and so I continued with my fact-checking.

Unfortunately, background checks and document retrieval only pay so much, and I was not the only guy providing this service. I found myself seriously struggling to make ends meet shortly after solving the Gonzalez murder case, and when you consider that I was living in a rented house in the tiny Panhandle town of Exile, you can see I was making almost no money at all.

So I began stripping away the luxuries, and as there were precious few of them I quickly got to cutting back on groceries. At first this fit in well with Mark's pull-up-the-drawbridge, half-rations-all-around siege idea, and I saw myself physically embracing the concept of a long campaign of denial. The potbelly flattened out, my office pallor turned into a nice Florida tan, and I felt I was finally making a stand.

I also relearned the standard college kid's tricks for stretching the food budget. It is amazing how a small piece of meat or fish can be expanded with rice or pasta, and you can get a lot of rice and pasta for very little money. The figure in the mirror continued to shrink, and with every lost pound I saw another small victory in the contest of wills.

In a strange side effect, my lowered caloric intake also led to less sleep. It wasn't that I had any trouble dropping off, or that I was having nightmares, but like the food intake, I simply didn't seem to need it as much. It worked in concert with my idea of a general simplifying of my existence, and it did not concern me at the time. The only real problem was the addition of unfilled hours which had formerly been dedicated to sleep, and so I went looking for a side job. A night job would kill two birds with one stone, taking up my slack time and providing me with more money, and so when I saw that the Midnight Taxi Service needed a night dispatcher I went over and applied.

I WAS DONE WITH THE TAXI service for the night, so I drove east through the moderately successful town of Bend-

ing Palms and on to my new home of Exile. The sun
was not yet fully up, and the gentle surface of the Gulf
of Mexico stretched away on my right as I drove. I was
renting a small one-story house a block or two from
the beach, and when I got back there I flipped on the
news to find that Manny was right about the cameras.

The local channel was jumping with the story of a
major drug bust at the Seaview Motel in West Davis,
and there was plenty of footage of the U-shaped concrete block motel. I recognized the district attorney
when he got up in front of the cameras and announced
the street value of the contraband found in the car of
one of the Seaview's guests, and then the shot switched
to earlier footage, probably shot the night before.

The Seaview was a pretty standard model motel that
I had seen in other parts of the country. It was cream
colored and two stories high, with an external metal
walkway running along in front of the doors on the
second floor. The doors were also metal, and they bore
the same red paint job as the railing. The main drag in
West Davis went right by it, so if you were standing in
the street you would be facing the parking lot. The long
side of the building ran parallel to the street, and the
two arms of the U shape came straight at it. The arm
on the left held the motel office, announced by a neon
VACANCY sign in the scene from the previous night.

The parking lot was jammed with police cars, and
the flashing lights bounced off the whitened walls of the
motel in a glaring series of flashes. The Seaview didn't

seem full up at the time, as there were more empty spaces than slots with cars in them, but then again Billy Lee had said everything had happened around eleven and so perhaps the other guests were out.

The scene flipped to a shot of a flatbed truck carting away a maroon four-door sedan that was comically decorated in yellow police tape. There was no footage of the suspect, but the D.A. came back on at this point, explaining that a forty-five-year-old office-supply salesman had been apprehended the night before. He had refused to allow Davis police to open the trunk of his car, and so the vehicle had been impounded. I assumed the drugs had been found at the impound lot, and began wondering just what had tipped them off when the D.A. answered me.

"The Davis police department received a complaint late last evening, a report of a car alarm that was sounding in the parking lot of the Seaview Motel. Upon arriving at the scene, Davis police officers were confronted by the suspect, one Ronald Baxter, a guest in the motel and the owner of the car. Mr. Baxter was behaving strangely, and when questioned by the officers became hysterical and needed to be restrained.

"Once Mr. Baxter had calmed down, he informed the officers that he was an office-supply salesman from Tampa, and that he routinely passed through this area as part of his marketing territory.

"The officers then asked to look in Mr. Baxter's car, and when Mr. Baxter refused this request he was placed in custody and his vehicle was impounded. A search conducted at the police impound discovered the drugs hidden within the body of the car."

He continued to speak, but Billy Lee's comments came back to me then. When he drove past the motel, the parking lot had been filled with police cars.

I was getting sleepy by then, and the story really had nothing to do with me at that time, but I did push off to bed wondering just why so many patrol cars had been summoned to a routine car alarm. This made no sense, even when the car's owner proved troublesome, and I nodded off with the vision of four police cruisers packing a small motel parking lot.

TWO

I AWOKE LATE IN THE afternoon, which was unusual because I was sleeping so little in those days. It was also unusual because my new girlfriend, a local photographer named Beth Ann Thibedault, normally tried to get by the house on her lunch break. Not that there was much intimacy yet, but she was the first person in my little circle to notice the decline in my waist and was making a decided effort to fatten me up.

Or at least she had tried. Of late I had begun to suspect she was growing weary of her mother hen role in my life, and the lack of a visit was not a good sign. It must have been a trial for her, waiting for some kind of resolution of my legal difficulties while at the same time fearing that just about any outcome would send me back up north. She owned her own camera store, taught photography at the local community college, and was not without options in the man department.

In the meantime, my choice of a night job had seriously curtailed the amount of time we could spend together and I also wondered if she suspected I still had feelings for my ex-wife, Lisa. I had told Beth Ann that I felt responsible for the failure of my marriage, blaming it on the long hours spent building up my business and then trying to save it, but I think she might have taken it the wrong way.

The news on the television was little more than a re-cycling of the earlier stories about the drug bust, and so after hanging around doing nothing for a couple of hours I headed in to work.

You HAD TO HAND IT to Mr. Corelli. He was a walking advertisement for good business sense. While he spared no expense when it came to the upkeep of the vehicles, he made up for the outlay by operating the tiniest taxi stand in the world. Sitting just inside the chain-link fence of the Midnight Service's parking lot, the stand itself was an octagonal hut barely ten feet across at any point. Its walls were a stack of concrete blocks topped by barred windows which ran all the way around under a corrugated tin roof. Ruby liked to say that it was sto-len from atop the wall of a local prison.

It was outfitted with a radio which could reach Mid-night cabs from there to Panama City (no small feat in a part of the world with that much water and lowland), a small refrigerator, a television, and a surprisingly ef-ficient computer. Corelli was a fanatic about logging in the fares, and even though the drivers did a pretty decent job of tracking their trips it was my job to make sure they were all recorded. Corelli had made a dark comment about tax evasion and money laundering when explaining the necessity of keeping accurate records, and I suspected he had encountered trouble in this area once before.

Corelli was a transplant like me, and had started driving a cab in New York City before he was old enough to hold a license. He had retired as the owner of three profitable cab stands sixty years later. Coming down to sunny Florida to enjoy his golden years, he'd practically gone nuts with nothing to do, and had started the Midnight Service in the name of keeping his sanity.

Even so, he was not loath to leave early, transferring the dispatch duties to Ruby or Manny until I got there for the night shift. Driving customers and doing dispatch at the same time was not an easy task and so I tried to be early as often as I could.

I had gained the drivers' grudging respect during the height of spring break a few weeks before. At that time I had been forced to get behind the wheel of a cab, handle dispatch, and drive fares around town, all the while keeping the log for the entire evening.

The next morning, the others had tried to help me check the log created under those circumstances and found it perfect. They were surprised by this, as I had spent much of the evening calling them for directions to places they knew by heart, and they had expected the log to be a similar disaster. (Of course I did not tell them about the tiny office assistant I had taped to the dashboard of my rig, or that I had learned to type like the wind on its tiny buttons while running my company up north.)

That evening I arrived at the Midnight lot, opened up the shack, canceled the forwarding of the phone, and warmed up the radio before calling Ruby to let him know I was there. The sun was still visible in the sky, and it was not a busy time for cab service, but Ruby seemed pleased to hear from me.

"Hey there, Frank. Nothin' much happenin' right now. You ready to copy?"

"Yes, I am. I am indeed," I answered breezily, wondering why we all started talking like interstate truckers when we got a radio microphone in our hands. The computer screen came alive as I typed in the record of three fares which had come and gone since Corelli had headed home.

"Tony's eating dinner at Del's, Manny's got a fare headed to the airport—"

"Was that called in?"

"No, that was a walk-on." Corelli was really strict about details like this. "And I am headed home as soon as I'm done with you."

Although spring break represented a spike in our business there in the Panhandle, things didn't really settle back down until well into the fall season. As a result, we had a rotating sleep cycle going that satisfied state regulations and still allowed us to put all of our drivers on the street most nights. The previous evening had stretched that system a bit too close to the legal norms, and so Ruby was going to be absent all night.

"Get a good night's sleep there, Rube."

"Who you callin' a rube, new guy?" he asked without heat and then signed off.

THE CABSTAND WAS IN A part of Davis dominated by office buildings, and so you might have expected us to have a more substantial presence than the simple dispatch booth. We got a lot of business from the surrounding buildings, and it seemed to make sense that we would have a bigger office and a few cabs right there to handle walk-up traffic. Both ideas were wrong.

Corelli had explained this to me during my first few days on the job. In the age of the cell phone, people would call a cabstand that was directly across the street from them rather than walk the entire twenty yards, even if the lot were full of taxis. At first I didn't believe him, but I began paying attention to the faces which walked by, and after a while I saw that they did not seem to notice that we were even there. It made me ponder the idea of hundreds of people in the surrounding buildings, dialing up the old dependable Midnight Taxi Service, without knowing the place was right around the corner.

The proximity of so many high buildings made the sunlight around the cabstand disappear prematurely each night. Even though that part of town cleared out early in the evening, I frequently saw people walking out of the office buildings late at night, and every now and then I caught some of the cell phone conversations as they headed to wherever their cars were parked. Most of the conversations were with angry spouses or disappointed children, and the constant refrain was that this was part of the job and there was nothing they could do.

While my personal circumstances were by no means ideal, my little window on the corporate world gave me a different viewpoint from the one I had held while running my company up north. Sad to say, my attitude about work had been very similar to the downtrodden souls who shuffled past the shack, and even worse, I had been the boss. Sometimes, late at night, sitting there looking out at the empty street and the superfluous buildings, I would speculate about whether or not my marriage would have survived even if my business had not died.

As a boss I had not been a slave driver, but the nature of software design demanded long hours and attracted people who did not like to leave problems unsolved. And as the boss, I had felt it was my responsibility to be there as long as anyone was still working. As a result, no matter how much time off I built in for people who had worked extra hours, I was usually at the office.

I know it is natural for someone in my reduced circumstances to look back at the unrewarded effort and feel resentment, but somehow I did not. I had honestly liked that business, and most of the people who worked for me had felt the same way. Only now, with the time and the quiet to look out the windows at other people in similar circumstances, was it all beginning to look like a tragically bad investment, or the gamble made by a fool.

IT WAS A QUIET NIGHT FOR the season, and I was engrossed in a book when the visitor walked up. He gave me quite a start. Walk-up traffic that almost never materialized during the day dropped off to zero after sunset. I shouldn't have been concerned, though, as the cabstand's blockhouse design was more functional than decorative, and I was well protected behind a locked security door and bulletproof glass.

The man who loomed up in front of me outside that window was tall, a black man wearing a nondescript outfit of dress slacks and a polo shirt. His short hair was mostly gray, and he had a light dress jacket slung over his arm in recognition of the heat. He spoke into the voice box in a tone designed to be nonconfrontational.

"Hello. My name is Curtis Winslow. I'm a private investigator from Atlanta and I was wondering if you could help me with something." He slowly unfolded a leather case showing his credentials and pressed them up against the glass, his face the picture of patience.

I had almost expected him to ask for directions (a common question at the stand during the day) but figured there was no reason for him to introduce himself for that. I took a moment to look at his credentials and noted that he worked for one of the country's bigger private investigations agencies.

"Sure. What is it?"

He returned the ID to his jacket pocket and brought out a letter-sized piece of paper, which he held up to the glass. It was a black-and-white copy of a high school yearbook photo showing a light-haired teenage male. I didn't know it just yet, but this was the kid who had flagged down Billy Lee's taxi the night before.

"I'm looking for a missing person. White male, twenty years old, caught a Midnight taxi a little to the west of here outside the Seaview Motel at around eleven o'clock last night."

My fact-checking job had brought me into contact with a large number of P.I.'s, and most of them were up-front about their methods. One of those methods is to create a pretext for talking to someone who might help them, a pretext which has nothing to do with the actual information they seek. So I would have been correct to be suspicious of the man standing before me, but I wasn't. Something about his demeanor suggested that he was genuine and that he had no need to fool me, but even so I decided to ask a couple of questions of my own.

"Does he have a name?"

"Dennis Taylor. Sound familiar?" Even coming through the speaker box his voice sounded deep, the voice of authority.

"Not really. You say he caught one of our cabs outside the Seaview last night?"

"Yes. I just came from there. The night clerk said he saw the kid leave the building when the police arrived. He saw him flag down the cab."

I felt that he was trying to get through the formalities quickly and I decided right then and there that he was on the level.

"Whaddya say we stop talking through the window? Come around back and I'll let you in."

He nodded his head as if appraising me, or maybe just in gratitude for a little courtesy after what had probably been a long day.

When he came through the door I saw that he was bigger than he had appeared in the window. There wasn't a spare pound on him. He shook my hand and accepted the stand's other chair, letting me hold the copy of the picture. It was actually a copy of a fax, which suggested he had gotten this assignment recently.

"You come all the way down here from Atlanta, Mr. Winslow?"

"Call me Curt." He took out a pocket notebook and a pen. "I flew down this afternoon. This one comes from one of our offices out west, the kid used the family credit card for his room at the Seaview Motel last night, and it was the first sign of him they'd had in days.

"May I get your name, please?"

"Sure. Frank Cole, night dispatcher." I took one of the Midnight Service's business cards from a stack on the desk and handed it to him. "Our number's on there."

"Thank you, Frank. Does any of this sound familiar to you? The taxi ride, I mean?"

He was actually asking if I had a record of the fare and where the kid went, but was trying to get there slowly.

"Well, I did hear about the drug bust, and one of our guys might have picked up a fare at that time, but right now it doesn't ring a bell."

I had no intention of misleading Winslow, but then again I had no intention of giving out Billy Lee's name without checking with him first. My own personal impressions notwithstanding, the Midnight drivers were a worldly bunch, and I was fearful of their reaction if I pointed one of them out to a stranger who claimed to be a private investigator.

"Any way you can check? A log, maybe?"

Winslow knew a lot more about the taxi business than he was letting on, and I began to see his method. He was one of those investigators who works all the way around a point just to gauge the reaction of the individual talking to him. Asking direct questions was certainly a way to go as well, but if it took the conversation to a dead end the questioner learned nothing. This way Winslow could always move into more focused inquiries if necessary, and also avoided the danger of scaring off a cooperative subject by coming on too strong.

"Yes, I can." I figured Corelli would want me to cooperate in a missing person case and that I would eventually end up giving this man what little information

I had, but I still wanted to check with Billy Lee. "I'm going to have to call my boss first, may take a while to get a hold of him…"

"That's fine." The quickness of his response told me he was the real item. He was experienced enough to know that I was going to make a couple of phone calls and didn't want him around to listen in. His willingness to allow that suggested he was nothing more sinister than a P.I. who had been running down strays for many years.

He stood up and stretched, and then took a long time yawning while taking a card out of his jacket. When I looked at it I saw that it contained his license number, and became even more convinced he was genuine.

"Go ahead and call whoever you need to. You think an hour will be enough?"

I nodded.

"Good. I'll be back in an hour. My cell number is on the card, too, if you get your boss before then." He stuck out his hand. "Anyplace good around here to eat?"

"OH, COME ON, FRANK!" Billy Lee's exasperated voice came over the phone at me. "A P.I. tracked that kid to my cab in twenty-four hours? That is flat-out impossible!"

"As I said, the kid's a runaway, used the family credit card at the Seaview, and the desk clerk saw him run out of there when he flagged you down. What's so impossible about that?"

"You think the clerk was still at his desk with all

those cops in the parking lot? Wake up, Frank. This guy is not looking for that kid."

"Then what is he looking for?" I asked slowly, genuinely dumbfounded.

"How should I know? You're the one who hangs around with these guys. They're never looking for whatever they say they're looking for."

"He had an awful lot of information about last night for a guy who's making it all up."

"No offense, Frank, but you're an easy mark. He probably walked up, got you talking about baseball and the taxi business, and before you know it you'd told him all about the kid and the cops and…hey, you didn't give him my name, did you?"

"No, I did not give him your name." I was getting hot by then. Billy Lee's reaction was hard to understand, but the assertion that I had blabbed the whole thing to the visitor was downright insulting, particularly after I had basically lied in order to make this phone call.

"Well, good! And don't! Listen, I'm due some vacation time and I'm taking it right now. Don't call my house 'cause I won't be there. Call Corelli and ask him what he wants you to do with this P.I., but don't mention me no matter what. Understand?"

"Not even a little," I answered, but he was already gone.

CORELLI TOLD ME TO DO exactly what I thought he'd tell me to do. I was to tell the P.I. that we had picked up a fare who might be that kid and tell him where he had been dropped off. I was not to give the P.I. anyone's name or confirm that it was the kid, and if he asked to speak with the driver I was to say that was against company policy. I was also supposed to ask the P.I. to come by in the morning once Mr. Corelli was in, and also tell him that we would comply with a formal request for information from the police.

Between Corelli and Billy Lee I felt like a nine-year-old.

Winslow came back ninety minutes later, looking fed and rested. He waved at me through the glass as he went by, headed for the back door, and I didn't have the heart to tell him no so I let him in again.

"That was a nice little diner you suggested, Frank. Thank you," Winslow said pleasantly as he sat down in the plastic chair he'd used before. "Any news?"

"Yes. I spoke with Mr. Corelli, the owner, and he said I could tell you about a fare last night that might be this kid. So here it is: One of our taxis picked up a fare outside the Seaview at eleven-fifteen last night and dropped him off at the Davis boardwalk at eleven thirty-five."

He nodded, not appearing disappointed in the least. The notebook was out again, and he wrote it all down slowly.

"Got a specific address for this boardwalk?"

I reached back onto the desk and took one of the Davis map sheets that we handed out to the tourists.

It was a basic street map with the more popular commercial attractions marked with numbered stars, and a big space in the corner showing the Midnight taxi logo and our phone number.

"The boardwalk runs from here to here," I said, showing the area already marked on the map. It was a one-mile segment of beachside jammed with restaurants and stores, quite popular during the warm weather. "No telling where he was actually headed."

"Did the driver say that?" he asked conversationally, not looking up from the map.

"No." Normally I would have been a bit more expansive than that, but my conversations with Billy Lee and Corelli had shut me up. "You can speak to Mr. Corelli tomorrow if you need more information. He told me to tell you that we'd cooperate with a formal request for information from the police."

I expected his attitude to change then, but it didn't. He was still looking at the map, and when he looked up it was with a tired smile.

"Twenty-five minutes to go ten blocks?" The Seaview was not on the map sheet, which meant he had a good idea of the area and had calculated the distance in his head. And I had to hand it to him for noticing that the total distance was just ten blocks. I sure hadn't. He stood up and extended his hand again as if I'd given him everything he'd ever need. I let him out, and he stopped in front of the voice box to make one more observation before taking his leave of me.

"Must be some heavy traffic around here late at night, to take that long to go such a short distance."

He looked at the empty street and walked off.

WINSLOW WAS NOT MY ONLY visitor that evening. Right around midnight the phone rang and a familiar voice asked, "May I get a taxi to bring a hamburger and fries to that scarecrow of a night dispatcher at the Midnight stand?" It was my girlfriend, Beth Ann, no doubt coming from the evening photography class she taught at Farragut Community College.

"I'm sorry, ma'am, we're not allowed to use our cabs for commercial deliveries. Are you going to be receiving some kind of payment for this service?"

"Oh, you bet, Midnight Cowboy." The voice disappeared abruptly, and Beth Ann's car raced past the booth and into a parking space in the Midnight lot. Although she owned the camera shop where she worked and ran a tight classroom at Farragut, Beth Ann had a definite wild side which showed up whenever she got behind the wheel. So careful in everything else she did, she drove with an almost total disregard for safety, and I tried hard not to let her take the wheel when we went places.

Despite that disquieting quality, I did like her a lot and was relieved to hear her in an upbeat mood about my eating habits. I was also lucky to have missed dinner and was actually ravenous, so I wasn't going to have any problem consuming that burger.

She came up to the back door as I hung up the phone, a twenty-five-year-old brunette wearing a sleeveless yellow cotton top and white shorts. She was carrying a large feed bag from some late-night food stand and a tray with two large sodas that were sweating in the heat.

I tried to kiss her, but she got the tray between us, pushing me back forcefully while raising the lunch bag over the tray with her free hand.

"Uh-uh, scarecrow. No sugar until you've eaten at least half of this." I took the bag, which was distressingly heavy, while she cleared some dispatch notes from the small side table and began removing the sodas from the carrier. To my relief, there were two complete burger-and-fry meals in the bag and I saw that she was going to eat with me.

"That's right, tiger. If you can't beat 'em, join 'em. I've gone on your ridiculous meal schedule, and once you see what it does to me you're going to start eating like a normal person again."

"I dunno about that," I said, still holding the bag and giving her the once-over. "Maybe a pound or two here or there might be just what the doctor ordered."

She hit me right between the eyes with the napkins, and I dropped the lunch bag on the desk before catching her up in my arms. She got her hands up at the last second, though, and pushed me away with alarming ease. Beth Ann had grown up on a farm, could shoot the ace of spades out of a playing card at twenty yards with a pistol, and at that moment I do believe she could have defeated me in a wrestling match.

"What did I say? Get eating."

We retired to neutral corners and started in on the burgers, which were covered in onions and astonishingly good after twelve hours with no food at all.

"So what's been going on here at Grand Central?" she asked between bites, looking around with a bobbing head at the still booth and the empty street.

"It's not that bad. I even had a visitor an hour or so ago." I began to fill her in on the story and she became animated once she learned that I had withheld information from Winslow.

"Do you think there's more to this? Like a few months ago?" I had tripped over the Gonzalez murder case while doing a background check for a local insurance business three months before, and had ended up solving the crime even though the culprit had escaped abroad. That case had started out as a simple hit-and-run, and clearly Beth Ann was seeing the same potential in the current situation.

"Oh, I don't think so. This one sounds like a basic runaway kid, and I'll bet Billy Lee is just being paranoid. The two things are probably unrelated."

"What do you think he's afraid of?"

"Not sure. I really don't know him well, so he might have this reaction to anybody asking questions. You know, the kind of guy who won't ever tell anybody his social security number even though it's the easiest piece of personal information to find. And the P.I. seems bored to tears with the case, so it's probably nothing."

"You should look into it anyway." She was staring at me intently, and I began to sense a serious turn to the conversation. I didn't answer, and she continued. "I mean it, Frank. You were really alive when you were looking at what happened to Eddie Gonzalez, and I think this would be good for you. Even if there's nothing there."

Beth Ann had known Eddie as a student at Farragut. He'd been run down while jogging one night over in Bending Palms, starting the whole chain of events that had led to my successful murder investigation. Beth Ann had not known him well, but there had been some ugly accusations about a possible link between some gambling at the college and Eddie Gonzalez's murder. Most of the faculty had been grateful when I proved the young man's death had nothing to do with illegal betting, at the college or anywhere else.

"You think so?" This was becoming my standard answer whenever Beth Ann tried to steer me toward eating more or dropping the taxi job. She'd even offered to pay my way until the fact-checking work picked up again, and I can't say I liked having these conversations.

She'd finished her sandwich by then, and even though I hadn't finished mine she stood up, wiping her mouth, and walked over to sit on my lap. We kissed, and she settled against me with her lips against my ear.

"I just want you to be happy, Frank," she murmured.

I hugged her hard, and she whispered, "Crazy about you, even if you are all skin and bones."

"You think so?" I whispered in reply.

IT MUST HAVE BEEN VISITING day at the cabstand, because I got two more before the night ended. Two more visitors, that is, not two more visits, as they came by together around four in the morning.

These two were interesting to look at, and they got a lot more interesting once they began talking. The tall one was probably thirty, maybe six feet in height with a full head of brown hair and a forehead full of lines. He was a beefy guy, and it was hard to tell if it was muscle or fat because he was wearing a subdued Hawaiian shirt untucked over a pair of dark brown trousers and running shoes.

His partner was medium height, balding, probably forty or so, and wearing a light blue tropical suit. From their getups I would assume the older one was supposed to appear to be management, but it got confusing as the conversation progressed.

"Hi there," the tall one started brightly, all teeth and friendliness. "Is this the Midnight Taxi Service headquarters?"

I had never thought of our mostly vacant lot and guard post as a headquarters, but I didn't want to be rude. Besides, it had been a long, dull few hours after Beth Ann left and these two seemed like a source of some entertainment.

"Sure is. You need a cab, sir?"

"Oh, no, that's not why we're here—" answered the older one, but the tall one cut him off almost immediately.

"Well, maybe we will, if you can help us." For the second time that evening someone pressed a picture of Dennis Taylor against the bulletproof glass of the booth's front window. It was actually a strip of pictures, the kind from a photo booth you'd find at an arcade, and this time Dennis had a friend. He had his cheek pressed up against the ringlet curls of a blond-haired teenage girl, and they both seemed quite happy.

"You see, Mr.—"

"Cole. Frank Cole."

The one in the Hawaiian shirt brought out a notebook and started writing in it.

"Coal? As in shovel?"

"Cole. As in slaw."

The one in the suit continued. "You see, Frank, we're looking for this gentleman right here and we have reason to believe he took a cab ride in one of your taxis late last night."

I was getting a very strange vibration through the window, and it made me just as prone to distrusting these two as I had been disposed to trust Winslow. Besides, I already had Billy Lee mad at me and this whole thing was getting weird enough to make me wonder if Billy Lee hadn't been right to be paranoid. I decided then and there that I wasn't going to help these two at all.

"Really? Does the gentleman have a name?"

"Yes, he does, Frank," the older one offered. The two of them were on either side of the circular voice box in the center of the glass, and it was hard to make out what they were saying through the vents. "His name is Dennis Sharp, he's a bail jumper, and we—"

"We just want to talk to him." The tall one cut in again. He smiled at me disarmingly, and nodded his head as he finished. "That's all."

"Bail jumper?" I looked hard at the photo. "He doesn't seem more than seventeen tops. That an old picture?"

"Yes, it is—"

It was the one in the suit's turn to interrupt.

"Not that old, though. That's exactly what he looks like. He's actually twenty-two, he's a con artist, and we need to find him." He nodded at me with a single bob of the head, one of those you-can-take-that-to-the-bank nods.

"You two bounty hunters or something?" I was starting to enjoy this. They had no way of knowing that I had been visited by Winslow and knew the kid's name wasn't Sharp. They also had no way of knowing that I'd done a few background checks on bail jumpers and was familiar with the laws governing their capture.

They were familiar with the law, too, though, and this was when the real performance began. Bounty hunting is illegal in Florida, and they practically went into a dance getting that across to me.

"Oh, no, absolutely not—"

"We are only trying to establish Mr. Sharp's whereabouts and possibly speak to him—"

"So that the bail officers involved in his case can also speak to him—"

"—and possibly resolve this situation without having to notify the local authorities."

They had my head going back and forth like a Labrador retriever watching a tennis match. The entire time they kept their voices high and friendly, almost comical in the intensity of their efforts, and between the smiles and the head nods I almost called the police myself.

The performance finally wound down and they stood there looking like a couple of hungry kids waiting for the microwave to stop turning, which was my cue to speak.

"You guys aren't from around here, are you?"

"What makes you say that?" the older one asked.

"Most people don't refer to their own police force as the local authorities. So where you from?"

"Hey, you are sharp as a tack there, Frank!" the tall one answered, as if we were all on the same team and enjoying a little locker room banter. "Actually, we move around a lot, do this sort of thing for a living, and so you're right. We're not from here, which is why we could really use any help you could give us."

"Well, I don't recognize him, but if you slip that

photo through the slot there I'll make a copy and see if any of the drivers know anything about this."

"Any chance we could talk to your drivers?"

I took the photo strip and walked over to the copier without answering them. The entire situation was becoming surreal, with so much excitement about what was nothing more than a simple taxi ride. I glanced at the window while the copier warmed up, and my two new friends were still standing there frosting the glass.

"Or maybe you could tell us. We also need to know if the kid was carrying anything when he flagged down the cab."

This was tricky. I was reasonably sure that Winslow wasn't out trying to flag down every Midnight cab in Davis in the hope of locating the right driver and having a nice little chat with him, but I couldn't put that past these two jokers if I simply told them off. And while I was pretty sure that Winslow was a law-abiding private investigator, I had no way of knowing if the guys on the other side of the partition were dangerous or not. I decided to get some more information out of them before trying my best to discourage them from approaching the drivers.

"Here you go," I said as I handed the photo booth print back through the slot. "What makes you think we picked this kid up?"

"He was at the Seaview Motel last night. The night clerk saw him flag down one of your cabs." The tall one said this, and I was grateful that they had stopped finishing each other's sentences.

"So why do you want to know if he was carrying something?"

"Oh, we're talking about a bag or a suitcase—"

"Anything that would indicate he was moving on—"

"Well, I'll ask around, like I said, but this doesn't sound familiar. You guys have a phone number?" It occurred to me that I didn't have a name on either one of them.

The older one produced a card and sent it through. It identified him as Harold Ames, with the name of a bail bonds office in Mobile underneath. The phone number had been lined through with a pen, and a new number was handwritten next to it.

"This you? Harold Ames?"

"Harry."

"Right." I picked up a pen and looked at the tall one. "And you?"

"Mark Knight. Call me Mark." I wrote it down.

"And is this the outfit you represent?" I held up the card, pointing to the name of the bail bonds operation under his name.

"Well, no, not this time, Frank—"

"In fact, that office went bankrupt a while back. That's why we're on our own. We used to work there." Back to the tennis match.

Now I had heard everything. They had given me enough information to get in touch with them, but not enough to confirm anything they'd told me. I did not doubt that the bail operation on the card probably existed at one time, but I would have bet my last dollar that these two never worked there.

"What did the kid do?"

"Excuse me?"

"What was he charged with when he jumped bail?"

"Check kiting."

"Low-level confidence games, pretty common stuff, really."

"Then why did the judge set bail for him?" I already knew where I was taking them, but it took them a few seconds too long to see it.

"Flight risk."

"Kid's got a record as long as your arm."

"I see." I looked down at the youthful faces on the copy paper. "But nothing big? Low-level stuff? Like you said?"

Harry almost saw where I was headed, but Mark was already nodding again and talking at the same time.

"Yep. Nothing to be concerned about. We just need to see if he'll go back on his own."

"Right. So how much you gonna clear on this one?"

I had them. They looked at each other for an instant, and Harry tried to salvage the story, but he knew it was already too late.

"Actually, we're doing this one as a favor—"

"Oh, I bet you are. After all, a kid this age, even one with a record, couldn't draw that high a bail for low-level stuff like you described. Most bondsmen I've met wouldn't send anyone looking for a skip unless it was big money. Really big money."

Mark bit his lower lip and looked at Harry, and Harry's face twisted with the effort of dancing around my argument. I decided to end the interview.

"In the meantime, if you were actually working for a bondsman, wouldn't you have a mug shot of this guy? Instead of a picture of him with his high school sweetheart?"

"That's a more recent photo—"

This time I did the interrupting.

"I'm going to give you ten seconds to get lost, and then I'm calling the cops." They started backing away. "And I'm calling all of our drivers to warn them about you. I got a good look at you, so unless you want to see the business end of some cabbie's handgun you better stay away from them!"

But they were already gone.

THREE

I DID CALL THE OTHER cabbies and tell them what had happened, even though I was reasonably sure that Harry and Mark, or whoever they were, had headed back to Mobile after scampering off. That is, if they actually were from Mobile.

Corelli was quite annoyed when I shook him out of bed for this, and told me not to report it to the police once he was sure the drivers had been warned. After a lifetime in the cab service he was leery of actively contacting the police about his business. He would gladly tell them everything that they asked him, but that was where he drew the line.

I thought this was a bad decision, but the phone conversation with Billy Lee and his subsequent vacation had lowered Corelli's opinion of me and he wasn't going to hear any of my arguments. Personally, I thought the Davis police would want to know about all the hullabaloo created by a runaway flagging down a cab at the site of a major drug bust, but Corelli said no and I dropped the idea.

The pointed question about whether or not Dennis Taylor, or Dennis Sharp, was carrying anything that evening had piqued my interest, though, and I decided to follow Beth Ann's advice and do a little looking of my own.

THE NEXT MORNING I WENT straight to the Exile Public Library after meeting the cabbies at the rest area. Ruby lectured me about giving strangers any information about the drivers, and like Corelli he wasn't willing to listen to my side of things. The others gave me the same cold shoulder I had experienced when we had first been introduced, and so I let them swab out their own rigs as I headed back to Exile. Though a small town, Exile had a big library with all the modern computer appliances, and I needed some time on the internet.

The library wasn't open that early in the morning, but that didn't mean no one was there. The research librarian, Mary Beth Marquadt, was a personal friend of mine and used to letting me in to use the computers for my fact-checking work. I had learned early on that Mary Beth liked to come to work well before normal business hours, and she opened the back door when I banged on it, letting me into the librarians' area.

"Good morning, Frank. Already hot as a June bug out there, isn't it?"

"You know it, Mary Beth. I didn't expect you to be in this early," I answered, in an effort to show that I did not take her presence for granted.

"Oh, you know me, Frank. You get this old, you sleep about five hours at most and then you might as well get up and do something useful." For all her talk about having nothing to do, Mary Beth was almost always busy no matter when she got to work. She was a better researcher than I'll ever be, and was in big demand among the town's schoolkids even during the summer.

She pointed me toward one of the open cubicles in the back office, which was something she could do only when we were alone. It gave me access to all of the internet tools the librarians used, which was a lot more than the normal machines out in the reference area. I also had access to a few of the investigatory databases on my own, as one of the law offices for whom I worked had bought me a subscription.

That was handy, as I wanted to confirm a few things about Mr. Curtis Winslow, Dennis the Menace, and my two buddies from Mobile. I started with Winslow, because I had the most information on him. I did not doubt his credentials in the least, but Billy Lee's suspicions had raised a question or two in my mind, and I hoped to confirm Winslow's bona fides before he met with Corelli.

It didn't take long to ensure that Curtis Winslow was exactly who he claimed to be, or that he was employed by one of the country's premier private eye firms. Having his license number printed on his business card made this easy, and I verified his credentials on the pay-to-use databases. Having accomplished that, I next went to the firm's website, where he had a substantial biography complete with a picture.

Winslow had started out as a police officer in Detroit some thirty years earlier and had moved on to private investigations work after earning his pension. The list of his service citations was extensive, almost all action decorations, and I made a note that this was one serious street cop. He was now based in Atlanta as he said, and his trail was so clean that I decided there was no reason to call Mr. Corelli. In fact, I doubted we would ever see Mr. Curtis Winslow again.

After doing that basic housekeeping, I did a haphazard search among the area's runaway reports using the name Dennis Taylor. I was not surprised to see this search yield nothing, as the kid had not been reported missing in the area and the family might not have even reported him at all. After all, the family credit card could have been canceled at any time, but they had left it open as a possible means of tracking the errant youth's travels. That sounded like a family that was trying to keep things low-key, and it fit well with Winslow's demeanor.

Then I did a search for the bail bonds operation on Harry Ames's business card and found that it had indeed gone out of business two years earlier. A reverse lookup on the phone number they had provided yielded nothing, but that was no surprise. Anybody worth his salt, investigator or criminal, can get a cell phone that is not listed in any directory and does not respond to caller identification, either.

The two phony bail guys seemed to be a real dead

end, and I was thinking that I really did need to give their information to the police when I remembered they had a different name for Dennis Taylor. Believing this to be as bogus as anything else they had said, I did a search for Dennis "Sharp" while listening to Mary Beth unlocking the main doors at the front of the building.

I slowly sat up when the search ended, and the first item returned was a large mug shot of the kid from the yearbook and the photo booth.

THE FACE ON THE SCREEN short-circuited me for a good while. His appearance as Dennis Sharp meant that Winslow didn't know his real name or was simply lying, and it also meant that the two bail bonds knuckleheads had at least been telling the truth about his real identity.

Reading further in the bulletin, an announcement that the kid was indeed a bail jumper, I learned that establishing this young man's identity was not exactly an easy thing to do. Apparently he moved around using a variety of pseudonyms, none of which was Dennis Taylor, and he had managed to convince more than one police department that he was nothing more than a simple vagrant.

Those departments had caught up with the truth later, when his fingerprints finally found a match with those of Dennis Sharp, but according to the bulletin he had already been released twice before that happened. I could only guess how many other times he had been picked up and released, times when the varied police databases across the country had not made the fingerprint match at all.

"You got to be some kind of talker to make an act like that work," I mumbled in the empty office, shaking my head as I read more.

My shaking my head not in amazement that he had escaped the clutches of the law in this fashion, but in a subdued form of admiration born of my own experiences in bankruptcy court. Speaking as a straight arrow who got run over by a judicial train that had jumped its own tracks to get me, I must confess a certain respect for the people who are nimble enough to dodge that train, even when they are guilty as sin.

Reviewing the charges against the kid, I felt the beginnings of a sort of kinship as I noted how many of his offenses were related to simple survival. He'd been picked up for vagrancy in Texas and had served ten days in a county jail because he could not prove he had a job or enough money to support himself. Following that episode, he had been cited in Louisiana for panhandling and had moved still further east. In Alabama he had finally committed a real crime, a traveler's check fraud scheme that sounded an awful lot like a case of barter gone bad. He'd given a false name while in custody that time, and managed to keep up the charade until released with a stern warning from the judge.

He'd crossed into Florida and next appeared near Miami, once again picked up for a traveler's check scheme. This one had been a bit more sophisticated than the offense in Alabama, and he had actually been tripped up by the value of the checks he was using, not their authenticity, as he had run afoul of money laundering regulations. He had posted bail as Dennis Turner that time, and once again the fingerprints had not caught up with him until he was out the door.

The bond had been minimal, though, and I seriously doubted that the bondsman who had floated the bail ever missed it. It was almost impossible that he had sent anyone looking for the kid. Skip tracing is expensive, and he probably wrote this one off to a fast-talking kid who was not what he seemed.

That was about the only part of this that bothered me. I could sympathize with a youngster trying to go it alone who was bumping into authority at every turn, but the kind of audacity required to pull this off is not found in the average runaway. Combined with the story Winslow had told me, with its worried parents and family credit card, I had to ponder just what I was looking at here.

The official record had him as twenty-four years old, but in all three pictures he looked seventeen. He was good-looking without being remarkable, and the record had him at five foot eight and one hundred fifty pounds. Even his hair was in that twilight range that catches the eye but does not draw real attention, listed as sandy brown instead of blond.

I needed more to go on here, so I kept at it despite my needing to go home and sleep. My fact-checking work mostly farmed the internet, and even though it is not rocket science you do need access to certain databases. It was usually a function of batting the information back and forth among those sources and then building on the hits that surfaced, and at the end of the process there was usually a tidy pile of data. Things like known associates, previous addresses, and even a credit history could yield important clues about an individual background or a current location in the case of a runaway like this one.

That process actually led me to trip over his parents, as I had not thought to go looking for them. While attempting to see if Dennis Sharp had done time in other states, I came across a Timothy and Winifred Sharp, entered together because they had been partners in a complicated confidence scheme which had landed them in two different prisons in Kansas. The con-artist angle fit what the phony bail bondsmen had said about the kid, but it seemed unlikely that this was anything more than three people with the same last name. I had to pursue it, though, and some further digging revealed the presence of a son named Dennis who was just outside the age limit which would have made him a ward of the state when his mom and dad relocated to Kansas.

The kindly faces which looked uncertainly into the mug shot camera could have belonged to any member of the PTA, but their individual criminal records told a different story. These two had been swindling people most of their lives, which led to an unanswered question about what their parents had done for a living. Eventually they had graduated to the big time, fleecing the kind of short-term, big money investors who had run my business into bankruptcy.

"Well, in that case they can't be all bad," I intoned quietly, fantasizing about my former backers entrusting their fortunes to people like the Sharps.

Trying hard not to feel more kinship with this obvious family of grifters, I printed out the supporting pages for what I hoped would be another interview with Curtis Winslow. Either he'd created a complex cover story to hide who he was working for, or Mr. Winslow was in for the surprise of a lifetime when I told him who he was actually serving.

INSTEAD OF GOING HOME and getting some rest, I got right back in the car and headed west. Telling Winslow that he was working for two inveterate con artists was one thing, but I wanted to know what was behind that line about a family credit card. Whoever had sent him down here had based their knowledge of Dennis Sharp's whereabouts on a credit card that clearly did not exist, and I needed to know just how the fledgling con man had rented his room that night.

Exile, in addition to being a small town, is far removed from the habitation of its neighboring towns. I whisked past long acres of tall pine trees as I went down the highway toward Bending Palms, and the heat rose up from the road in waves.

I had always liked the tall, slender pines down here, but for the first time I noticed the varied colors of the undergrowth beneath them. It was a mishmash of purple, yellow, and green, none of it more than a foot tall, and it put me in mind of the low-level hustler who had started this strange chain of events.

I had always overlooked this mass of multicolored undergrowth because of the trees above it, and it seemed a good analogy for the below-the-radar existence Dennis Sharp had been leading. The vegetation was vibrant and colorful if you actually looked at it, but if you focused on the pines you were likely to miss the whole show. It seemed to open my mind, and the many possible explanations for my current puzzle rebounded in my head as I went.

Perhaps Winslow had not been hired by the Sharp family after all. With Mom and Dad in jail, Sharp Junior had been out on his own and doing what appeared to be a poor job of making his way. Perhaps he had offended someone not mentioned in the police reports, someone who had contacted Winslow's agency with a bogus story about concerned parents and a family credit card. That explanation fit my idea of Winslow, but it didn't explain how the concerned parties knew the kid had taken a taxi ride the night before. If they were close enough on his tail to know that, why would they call in a private eye from Atlanta?

This raised yet another possibility, the chance that the kid hadn't had a room at the motel at all. His record suggested he was comfortable living as a street person, and motel rooms cost money. They also create a trail of desk clerks who might remember your face, or see you hop a cab while the police are packing as many cruisers as possible into your motel's parking lot.

Bending Palms is bigger than Exile, with a more vibrant business community and an actual main street flanked with stores, but it wasn't that big and I was through there and into Davis before I knew it.

Davis is a subdued rich man's land, with enough glitz to hold its head up but not enough to look as if they're really working at it. Although much of this money is transplanted from other parts of America, it had mingled well with the locals and adopted their inconspicuous ways. The place did have two marinas, a dozen motels, three beaches, and a boatload of businesses, but if you knew just how much money is based in Davis you'd be surprised that it doesn't show more.

Then again, a little farther to the west is the vacation paradise of Panama City and perhaps the denizens of Davis felt they had all the hopping nightlife they'd ever need over there. I'd spent a spring break in P.C. one college year, and had fallen in love with the place right off the bat. The motels and clubs were right on the beach, the sand was an amazing white color, and there were weekends when you thought every beautiful young woman in America had donned her bathing suit and come there to hang out.

Although Panama City was more touristy than Davis,

it was an upscale kind of tourism and if you didn't have a lot of money you were better off getting a room in West Davis. I passed through the trendy shopping district of Davis proper and hit West Davis with the usual feeling of having made a wrong turn.

You didn't need a map to know you'd passed out of the promised land when you got to West Davis. Cheap motels, pawn shops, used-car lots, tattoo parlors, and even a couple of strip joints beckoned from both sides of the main drag, a road which had been selling Rolex watches and BMW cars not more than a mile back. Still, the place wasn't all that bad, considering it was the bad part of town, and the crime rate was actually quite low.

I rolled up to the Seaview Motel and parked on the street instead of going straight into the parking lot. The U-shaped two-story motel was emptying out even though it was still early morning. A maid in street clothes was pushing a cart along the upper tier, knocking on the dull red doors and entering the empty units when there was no answer. A large transparent trash bag hung from the cart, a mop handle showed above the rim, and a stack of clean linen was attached on the side opposite the trash bag.

The parking lot was big enough to contain thirty cars, but there were only three present at that time. Two were rolled up facing the ground-floor doors and a third was sitting out in the middle of the lot where it was just possible to make out the old painted lines of overflow spaces. The arms of the motel reached out on either side of the parking lot, and the cream-colored arm on the left had the word OFFICE painted in big letters on it.

Walking up to the office, I had to pick a pretext for being there asking questions. On any other day I would have used the absolutely true story that I was with the Midnight Taxi Service and that we were trying to find a young man who had hailed a taxi outside the Seaview two nights before. That day, however, I was in hot water with Corelli and Billy Lee, and wasn't going to take any more chances with the Midnight name.

There are many good reasons not to pretend to be someone you are not when you are trying to get information, and the two phony bail bondsmen had demonstrated one of those reasons a few hours earlier: It's too easy to get caught. And no matter how pure your motives, once you've been caught lying to a clerk, a neighbor, or a passerby who might have seen something, you can forget about ever getting that information.

There are also legal ramifications to consider, and I knew my buddy Mark in New York would not appreciate my getting picked up for impersonating a police officer, a private detective, or even an insurance adjuster. I'd used the insurance cover once before, but I had been working for the Sun Provident Mutual Assurance insurance company at the time and so it had not really been a lie. I am sure that the Sharp family (currently of Kansas) or their streetwise offspring would laugh at this, but then again I bet they could pull it off every time. I was not as confident of my own abilities, and so I decided on the simplest route possible.

I walked into the office, a cramped space filled with a paneled front desk, an ATM, a coffee machine, and an ancient arcade game in which the player tries to snag a variety of worthless toys using a mechanical arm. The air-conditioning was turned on high, and a man wearing black plastic eyeglasses was seated behind the desk reading the morning paper. Following my chosen "cover," I went up and placed Dennis Sharp's graduation picture on the counter.

The simplest way of getting information, I had discovered, is to say nothing. It works every time.

The man behind the counter, who was wearing a short-sleeved white dress shirt embroidered with the name of a Panama City motel on the pocket, turned down one side of the newspaper long enough to look at the picture and then snapped the paper back into place.

Well, sometimes the simplest way takes two tries, but I still said nothing as I laid a second picture alongside the first. This got his attention: It was a printout of the police bulletin describing Dennis Sharp as a low-grade fugitive. The kid stood in front of several horizontal lines indicating his height, and the universal recognition of a mug shot did the trick.

"I knew it. I just knew it." The man folded up the paper and stood up, revealing that he was quite tall and quite thin. I would guess he was forty at most, but he gave off the frustrated air of someone who has dealt with a few hundred vacationing college students too many. He picked up the bulletin and began reading. A few moments later he looked at me for the first time and asked, "You gonna catch him?"

"More like 'catch up' to him, actually." I smiled thinly. That was as close as I was going to have to get to saying I was a bounty hunter.

"Any chance of us getting restitution when you do?"

"Probably not restitution, but there are some people looking for this guy—"

"No kidding. You're the fourth one since that little thief ran out on his bill." So much for the story about the family credit card.

"—and if you give me information that helps me catch up with Mr. Sharp there, I am authorized to reward you." I looked at a large sign informing the office guests that all rooms went for forty-five dollars a night, and decided to stretch the truth just a little. "How's a hundred dollars sound?"

"That would be very nice," he said, as if already imagining that money disappearing into his back pocket. He plucked a business card from his shirt and handed it to me. "Number's on the card. Now, what do you need to know?"

He hadn't given me his name, and I didn't ask for fear that it might lead to identifying myself unnecessarily, now that my Mysterious Stranger act was going so well. I glanced at the card briefly while tucking it into my empty wallet and saw the name Roger Canfield in the dead center.

"These other three. One was an older African-American, a private investigator named Winslow?" He nodded. "And the other two were working together—"

"I didn't get to talk to the other two. They came by last night, while I was eating dinner. My assistant talked to them."

"Is your assistant here right now?"

"No, he went off duty a few hours ago. He'll be here this afternoon around four, if you want to talk with him."

I pulled out a pen and notepad, more for effect than a belief that I would have to come back to talk with his assistant. In fact, I had only asked about Winslow and the two bail bonds knuckleheads to establish myself as already knowing everything, so I decided to keep things moving.

"Probably not necessary." I tapped the mug shot sitting on the counter. "This one here usually uses bad traveler's checks to get around. Is that how he paid for his room?"

"Nope. He was carrying a stolen credit card. My assistant was on duty when he checked in, and I'm sorry to say this Sharp fellow talked his way around him. Some sort of story about the card belonging to his stepfather."

"That works?"

"Oh, you'd be amazed at how many young people we get down here who run out of money and fall back on Dad's credit card. You get pretty used to it. Half the time we don't even call to make sure it's all right." Calling meant long distance charges.

"So you have a credit card receipt?"

"Well, no, not really. You see, my assistant tried to run the card through the checker, but he got this funky error message back. Happens sometimes, just means the line's down for an hour or so." Roger stopped looking at me and his sentences picked up speed. His tone hadn't changed, but he sure seemed to be lying.

I didn't consider it noteworthy, though, because I believed I was hearing one of many excuses used by the Seaview's manager when the monthly accounts didn't balance. With my background in the technology business, I was well acquainted with people who seized on minor mechanical glitches to explain away problems which had nothing to do with the machinery.

"So he gave him a room anyway."

"Yes, he did." He looked up suddenly. "He's a good guy, works real hard, and he was actually watching for that kid to run out on us, that's why he saw him flag down that taxi."

Although the credit card story was getting muddier by the minute, at least I now knew that the part about the night clerk seeing the kid wave down Billy Lee was true. I was still staring at Roger, and he went on.

"Hey, he even put him in the room right over the office so he'd know if the guy went out. Just wasn't fast enough to stop him, is all."

I've never run out on a bill in my life, and yet I could see a hundred ways a determined kid could get around that one. Mentally remarking at the lengths to which the manager was going to defend his assistant to an unconcerned bounty hunter, I moved on to the topic which really concerned me.

"How about this drug bust? The kid have anything to do with that?"

"Oh, I doubt that. He ran down the stairs and right by the door there just a few minutes after the police arrived."

"Your assistant saw that?"

"Saw what?"

"The kid running by."

"Yeah. I was already out in the parking lot trying to find out what was going on." He looked uncertain for an instant. "You see, I was eating dinner when the kid checked in, but I had come back by then."

I wrote it down even though it sounded like more nonsense.

"So which room was the drug guy in?"

"Number twenty-one, last ground-floor room opposite the office here." He pumped a thumb in the direction of the parking lot. "You think this kid was really involved with that?"

"You never know. He sure cleared out of here fast once the lights started flashing, didn't he?"

"Well, that was probably about the credit card more than anything else."

"Probably." I shut the notebook and clicked the pen closed, watching to see if a look of relief came across his face. It did, and so I decided to run him just a little further. "This credit card. It didn't go through the first time, but your assistant gave the kid a room anyway."

"Right."

"So did he keep the card? So he could run it through later? When the machine was done hiccuping?"

He seemed relieved to be back on Motel Manager ground.

"Oh, no, that's not necessary." He pulled open a narrow drawer and began going through what looked like several hundred blank postcards. "He would have made an impression of the card and tried typing in the information later. Here we are."

He brought up a guest sign-in sheet, partly filled out by Dennis Taylor on the night in question, and stapled to it was a standard credit card receipt. It was unsigned, but it showed the information for a major credit card agency and a card issued to one Lawrence Chambers. I wondered just how Dennis Sharp, traveling as Dennis Taylor, had talked his way around that one.

"May I get a copy of that?" I asked. Looking into the dull eyes of the head manager, I decided that the young con artist had run circles around the night assistant without even breaking a sweat. Dennis had spun a yarn about Uncle Larry giving him his credit card and telling him to go wild in sunny Florida, and that had been that.

He asked me about the one hundred dollars as I stepped out into the sun, and I gave him a reassuring smile before letting the door swing shut. I took a quick turn into the parking lot and looked up, seeing the motel room directly above the office, the one that Dennis Sharp had rented. Turning around, I looked straight across the parking lot at the first-floor door directly across from Sharp's room, the room rented by the drug guy.

"Nice view, Dennis," I said out loud.

FOUR

I WENT TO WORK EXTRA early that evening, and Corelli said he had sat down to a nice chat with Mr. Curtis Winslow. Corelli knew all about my other job and assumed that I had checked Winslow's credentials in my spare time, so when I confirmed this he added his own opinion that Winslow was a straight shooter. I did not bother telling him about the other things I had learned about the kid, as Corelli obviously felt the Midnight Service had seen the last of Dennis Sharp and at least two of his pursuers.

As for the pretend bail bondsmen, they had not resurfaced yet, at either the cabstand or with one of the drivers. By this time Corelli's annoyance at my behavior the night before had transferred to Billy Lee, who was not at home and apparently intended to be gone for some time. Having met Winslow, Corelli had decided that Billy Lee was putting everyone in a bind over some foolishness he had invented in his head. He had told Winslow about the fake bail guys, and Winslow had said he had not run across them.

Corelli did say that Winslow wanted to see the photo booth picture of the kid and his girlfriend, and that the P.I. would be by sometime early that evening. That pleased me, as I had a bomb I was going to drop on him and would have had to call him otherwise. After Corelli went home I called up the drivers in a general broadcast on the radio and warned them to be on the lookout for both the kid and the bail guys, an admonition that got me a torrent of scorn that lasted a full minute.

"Hey, Frank, there's a suspicious old guy sitting on a park bench across the street from me. He's been there all day, seems to be cooking up some kind of scheme with the pigeons. Should I call the cops?"

"Frank, I forgot my sunblock. Can I go home?"

"Hey, can I just stop giving rides to males under thirty, and every male over thirty? That would be cool!"

"Which way does the ignition key turn again? I forget."

"I'm not going into West Davis without Frank."

Manny finally shut them up, even though he'd delivered at least one of the gibes himself. The radio cooled off, and I exhaled loudly.

"If you only knew," I said to myself as I pushed the stand-up microphone across the desk.

Winslow showed up before it got dark, pulling a red rental car right into the Midnight lot and coming straight to the back door of the guardhouse. He was a bit more awake than when I had last seen him, and he appeared to have something on his mind. He was still wearing the dress slacks and collared shirt outfit, and he walked across the lot with a purpose.

"So, Frank. Were you going to tell me that you and I

are in the same line of work, or was I supposed to guess that?" he asked in a friendly manner, shaking my hand. A slight smile curled the corners of his mouth as he sat down, and I figured that expression was going to evaporate in less than a minute.

"I'm just a fact-checker. And as you can see—" I indicated the surroundings with two upraised hands "—not quite good enough at it to make ends meet. So tell me, Curt. Who does the background checks for you up in Atlanta?"

"Oh, we have a whole bunch of folks who do that part of the job, Frank. Sorry I can't use you."

"Sure about that?" I handed him the printed police bulletin about Dennis Sharp, and he practically fell out of his chair. The smile definitely disappeared, and his mouth even hung open for a second as he read. One thing seemed apparent: He had not known that Dennis Taylor was Dennis Sharp.

"Where'd you get this?" he whispered, glancing up with a look of pain similar to that worn by people who lost a big bet at the track. He offered the names of two large criminal background databases, and I nodded once because I had used them both.

"Sharp?" he asked after a moment, still in disbelief.

"That's his name. As you can see, he gets around. Taylor's not one of the listed aliases, but that probably doesn't matter. The point here is you've been looking for a runaway with a different name. So who set you on this trail?"

"I was not lying to you, Frank." Now his eyes were large, and they bored into me. "And I'd bet big money that no one in my office was lying to me, either. I was proceeding on the information given to me, and the parents are in another state so I didn't meet them."

"I hate to do this to you, Curt, but you're right about the other state. Kansas, actually." I handed him the two mug shots of Timothy and Winifred Sharp, and for an instant there he looked as if he were going to have an aneurysm. Getting bad information was one thing, but being played by a couple of cons was completely un-acceptable in his business. He muttered a few curse words as he read, but that was the extent of it. He took some time reading the parents' information, and the storm had passed by the time he was finished. When he looked up, it was with the demeanor of a guy who has heard he has three months to live and only wants to know if that is a hard number.

"You found this on the internet?"

"Yep." I gave him a quick rundown of my search procedures, and he asked a couple of questions which told me he was familiar with the technical part of the job. He went quiet again for a while at that point, and I let him try to put it all together in his head before ask-ing the obvious question.

"You going to call your office and find out what's really going on?"

He looked up at me as if I were some kind of idiot, and when he replied it was with great certainty.

"Have no doubt about that, Frank. I am going to run this thing down to whoever first brought this into the firm. You got any idea what kind of lawsuits they opened us up to, if we are in fact working for a couple of cons? Cons who are currently inside?"

"Well, I don't know what the truth is here, but you might consider the possibility it isn't them. Maybe the kid made some high-powered enemies along the way, somebody who's impersonating his parents. Maybe they're not involved at all."

He cocked his head to one side as he chewed on that one, and a couple of lines vanished from his forehead.

"You're better at this than you think, Frank. That might work, too. I was told about the motel when I got assigned to this case, and they said that was based on the kid's use of a family credit card…" He went on to say a couple of uncomplimentary things about the staff at the Seaview, now seeing that the story about the family credit card had been bogus. "You know, I didn't even check to see if he used a credit card at all."

Normally I wouldn't have been too sure about rubbing a stranger's face in something like this, particularly someone his size, but my recent thumping at the hands of the Midnight drivers had left me cranky. I also hadn't cared for his automatic assumption that I was looking for a job with his firm. I had done about one hundred percent of the fundamental investigating that Winslow and his office should have done, and so I let him have it.

"I did. He used a stolen card and talked his way around the night clerk." I handed him a copy of the credit card receipt, and he slumped a little more in his chair.

"That means everything I was told was a lie. The only accurate thing I've discovered here is that the kid flagged down a cab." He shook his head, the smile having returned, and he stuck out his hand once more. He spoke as we shook. "Frank, if anyone asks, you have been working as a contract fact-checker for me for the last twenty-four hours. We have a flat fee of two hundred dollars for this kind of contract job, but if you have an actual rate I'll see we cut you a check in that amount."

I beamed, forgetting my pique of a moment earlier. Beth Ann had been right about the job's effect on my general outlook, and receiving this kind of recognition from a professional added tinder to the spark. Besides, I needed the money. Winslow seemed to understand, looking over my shoulder toward the file on the desk which had produced all the information so far.

"So. What else you got in that magic file of yours?"

FOR THE SECOND TIME, Winslow was the harbinger of unexpected visitors, and even though this visitor was on my cell phone he was certainly unexpected. It was my lawyer buddy Mark, calling from New York with what I hoped was good news.

He didn't call all that often, as he was accustomed to

the glacial pace of the court system and only reported actual developments, but I still experienced a mad rush of hope whenever I recognized his voice on the line. Although I had been down in Exile for over a year and there had been little indication of impending resolution of my case, somewhere inside me an irrational software guy still believed it was all going to be put right someday.

Not that day, it turned out. Mark's voice on my cell phone sounded high-pitched and distant there in the booth, and I hoped I wouldn't get any calls for a cab for a few minutes.

"Hey, roomie. How's the weather?" Mark was always upbeat, no matter how bad his news usually was.

"The usual. Sun's gone down and still hot as an oven."

"I bet. Listen, I'm gonna fly down there this weekend to visit. Don't get your hopes up, but there's been a development I can't talk about over the phone."

"Mark, I don't think anyone's intercepting this call." I had no way of knowing that, but I sure didn't want to wait three days to find out what he knew. "Give it to me. What's happened?"

"Hey, I'm not kidding, tiger. This is gonna have to wait until I can say it to you in person. It's not much, but it throws things into a whole different kind of light."

Just before I asked what that meant, I remembered the ghostly phone call I had received just a week earlier. Just after I arrived in Exile I got the first of these calls, a monthly wrong number with no voice on the other end, and I had always assumed it was my creditors up north, just letting me know they were watching. The call always came at around one o'clock in the morning, and it only happened once of an evening. When I got sick of it and went to the phone company, they were unable to trace the number.

Last week's call had been a little different, though. I had been shaken from a deep sleep, one of the few real periods of slumber I'd enjoyed since I'd dropped the weight, and this time there had been someone at the other end of the line. It was a man's voice, deep and amused, a sadistic prison guard opening the slit to a darkened solitary confinement cell. He'd only said the one sentence, but it was enough.

"How's it goin' down there, Frank?" he'd asked, and then the line had gone dead. The phone company hadn't been able to track that call, either, and remembering the call I started to think that perhaps Mark was right. Besides, I could use the visit.

"Can you give me a hint?"

"Sure," he said reluctantly, and then that supercomputer mind of his whipped out an answer. "You know the goodies our mutual friend is holding? It's about them."

The mutual friend was an insurance company in Hartford that had been forced to eat a huge payout when my business died, and the goodies were the software patents that had been mine but were now theirs. The rights to those inventions were now gathering dust in a drawer, as the insurance folks had no way to sell them and were holding them against the unlikely chance that I would someday strike it rich again. My former partners had not displayed much interest in gaining control of these items during the bankruptcy, but in recent months Mark has begun to suspect this had changed.

"Those goodies aren't exactly fresh," I offered. Software innovations don't have a long shelf life, and I had already seen reverse-engineered versions of some of those processes out on the market, so I had to wonder what the interest could be.

"As if anybody could ever tell what our friends were after," Mark offered, sounding frustrated for the first time since he had taken the case. A year ago he had been quite optimistic that a settlement or an appeal would eventually work out for us, but this latest scrap of news suggested otherwise. It sounded as if my old partners were asking for the one thing I couldn't give them, and that they were digging in for the long haul. A long siege.

The cabstand phone rang then and I had to answer it.

"That's a customer calling. Let me know when you're arriving and I'll come get you."

"In a cab?"

Despite the dark nature of the conversation, I still had to laugh. I told him off the way that old college roommates do, and ended the cell phone call. Reaching for the real phone, I paused to consider what he'd said. A long siege.

I looked down at my diminished waistline and wondered just how far into that siege I would last.

THE NEXT MORNING WAS A moment of reckoning. Winslow had called an hour after Mark had hung up, just to let me know he was headed to Kansas City for an argument with someone very high up in his firm. He'd tried to get to the bottom of things from his motel room in Panama City, but it hadn't worked and he believed he was going to have to "get insistent." That was the phrase he had used, and I decided I was better off not knowing what he meant. He promised to be in touch, and I decided to get insistent myself with some people who'd been giving me a hard time.

I picked up the coffee a little early that morning and was waiting at the rest stop when the first Midnight cab rolled up. I felt a shot of adrenaline freeze my arms when I recognized the rig as Manny Batista's, but I steeled my nerve and took a good hold of the garden hose as he got out and approached.

I had attached the hose to the spigot, placing the coffee tray next to the corroded standpipe that stuck up out of the picnic area's grass. I was sitting down in that same grass as Manny walked over, looking bewildered at the coffee's location.

I sprayed him without saying a word, and he jumped back in surprise. It was a short burst, but it soaked the front of his shirt and he let out a brief yell before fixing me with The Stare.

I stared right back at him, and he stood there for ten seconds or so before figuring it out.

"Now, Frank, you gotta expect a little hazing in a job like this—"

I sprayed him again and he backpedaled a few steps, the hands at the ends of those bulging arms balling up into angry fists.

"Now, cut that out! I'm gonna have to go home and change! Stop being such a baby!" I tried to spray him again, but he was out of range by then. Thankfully, the temperature was already almost seventy and he'd dry out in no time, but right about then I'd had enough of the Midnight crew's idiosyncrasies.

"What's this about, Frank? Really? Is it Billy Lee?" Manny was trying to reason through my strange behavior without resorting to violence, and another rig came down the road as he waited in vain for a reply. Tony Ng parked his cab almost on the grass so he could get a good look at what was going on, and when he stepped out it was with a look of amusement.

"Hey, Frank, you're supposed to hose out the cabs, not the cabbies!" he called from a safe distance. "Whatsamatter, Manny? You get a little on you? Guy was leanin' in the window when Frank called?"

Manny unclenched his fists and shook his arms, sending droplets in all directions. He wasn't laughing yet, but at least he didn't look as if he were planning to blacken both my eyes.

"Laugh now, Tony, but look where he's got the coffee. And he won't say what's wrong."

"Won't say what's wrong? Frank, keeping your complaints to yourself is against Midnight company policy. Just ask any of the drivers. Now, what do you say we all shake hands—" I almost got him with a long, arching shot that he dodged just as Ruby's van pulled in. I hadn't expected the senior driver to be there that morning, and there was a chance that this development could have repercussions for my job.

"Oh, you're in trouble now, Yankee! Ruby's here. You gonna hose him, too?" Manny called out in a laughing singsong. He pulled the long shirt over his head to reveal an impossibly hairy chest that was much more defined than I had thought. I was doubly thankful that I hadn't riled him enough for real trouble.

Ruby walked toward me slowly, taking in the scene as the sun began to appear on the horizon. Manny started to wring out his shirt while Tony began alternately pointing at me and at his head to signify that I had lost my mind, but Ruby kept on coming in a rolling, side-to-side waddle.

He stopped just outside of range and said in a clear, soft voice, "I apologize for treating you with disrespect, Mr. Cole. The Midnight Service works hard at creating a friendly and accommodating workplace, and if I have offended you in any way I take it back." He doffed the porkpie hat in as much of a courtly bow as he could manage, and fixed me with big sad eyes.

"Come get your coffee, Rube," I said, still glaring at the other two.

He waddled forward, identified his cup from the markings made at the coffee stand, and straightened up with an audible pop from the bones in his back. Peeling back the lid, he looked at Manny and Tony and asked, "You guys gonna stand there all day or you gonna say you're sorry?"

They both mumbled something at me, and I lowered the nozzle just as Danny's van rolled in. Manny and Tony both approached warily, getting their coffees and regarding me with unease while Danny got out of his rig, walked over, and took his morning java from the carrier.

"Uh, Frank, why didn't Danny have to apologize?" either Tony or Manny asked from behind me as I began screwing the faucet shut. I turned and stared at both of them.

"Since when does Danny say anything bad to anybody?"

MY MAIN PURPOSE IN HOSING down my coworkers that morning was to get their attention. They had been so focused on Billy Lee's antics and their own belief that the runaway kid was long gone that they hadn't taken my warnings seriously, and with my new information I couldn't let that condition continue.

I had secured a group pledge to be extra aware of their customers by the time we split up that morning, as the new wrinkle of the Sharp family's criminal past now raised the outside chance of danger to an actual possibility. More to the point, we just had no idea what had hopped into Billy Lee's cab that night, or what was chasing him.

I didn't bother telling them that Dennis Sharp's motel room had provided a bird's-eye view of the drug runner's room simply because I didn't want to get them going again on my raging paranoia. Even so, the real chance that the kid was involved with drugs and drug people had concerned me enough to risk getting seriously injured by a gang of damp cab drivers.

I got a promise from them to watch out for Dennis Sharp as well, hoping that their travels might bring them near him in the teeming mass of young people that is the Panhandle summer, and handed out copies of his picture. Driving away, I honestly thought there was a chance that we might locate the kid and have him sitting in the Davis jail before Winslow got back.

Of course, I didn't know the kid was dead then, but I found out soon enough.

A LOUD BANGING ON MY screen door woke me with a start just after noon. I had every window and the front door open to let out the heat, and whoever was doing the banging did not have to do it twice.

I lurched down the entire five feet of hallway that

separated my bedroom from the living room, and was relieved to see the familiar black face of Denny Dannon, Exile's chief of police, standing on my porch. Dannon was in the full gray uniform of the three-man Exile police force, with a tan park ranger's hat set level just over his sunglasses. He looked official, and somehow I knew the Sharp case was about to come back on me.

"Come on in, Chief. I was asleep. You want coffee?" Dannon and I had grown close in my year in Exile, largely because he felt bad about opposing my involvement in the Gonzalez case a few months before, and so he knew all about my night job. He took his hat off as he crossed the threshold, a habit from his hitch in the Navy shore patrol many years earlier, and for the first time I saw he was holding something. It was a file folder, and for a brief instant I hoped that my investigative sideline might be picking up.

"No, thanks, Frank, but go ahead and set yourself up." He followed me into the tiny kitchen adjoining the living room, and I began running water into a tea kettle. I was wearing a bathing suit and a T-shirt, and I could feel his eyes trying to guess how much (or how little) I weighed. Though tall and lean himself, Dannon didn't have any trouble telling a healthy physique from one that needed a meal.

"Frank, I got a call from the police over in Davis, and they'd like to talk to you about some questions you've been asking." He spoke in a normal conversational tone, and since the Sharp case was the only thing I had going on I knew what he was getting at.

"This about a runaway named Dennis Sharp?"

"Yeah." He seemed uncertain for an instant, watching as I turned on the stove and set the kettle on the burner. I looked at him with a face more marked by sleep than concern, and so he just let it out. "Frank, the kid's dead."

DANNON HAD BROUGHT ALONG a set of faxes he'd received from the police in Davis. One was a copy of the police bulletin which I already had, and the other was an initial coroner's report which said that the John Doe now identified as Dennis Sharp had been shot once in the chest with a .38 caliber handgun at close range. Time of death was estimated at between five and ten hours after the drug bust at the Seaview, although the connection to the Seaview was in my head only. Calculating how long Sharp had been gone, I marveled at how many people had been looking for a dead guy for the last two days.

A hiker had found the body off to the side of a trail in one of Davis's recreation areas, a large stretch of woods known as a good spot for teenagers to go be teenagers. Although the Gulf region has its share of runaways and muggings, an out-and-out murder is quite unusual in my neck of the woods, and the Davis cops had processed the kid pretty quickly. The body had been near an old maintenance shack, and a search of the area had yielded a small backpack with what seemed to be Dennis Sharp's earthly belongings. The backpack's contents had provided few clues regarding Dennis Sharp's final hours, but a crumpled Midnight Taxi Service map in the kid's pocket had suggested he had recently taken a cab ride.

Though a long shot, they had called the cabstand and hit pay dirt. Corelli had practically lost his mind at the way this simple fare was consuming his life, and he had told the Davis cops everything he knew. Presumably they were trying to locate Billy Lee while I was talking to Chief Dannon, but they were particularly keen on talking to me.

They probably got my phone number from Corelli as well, but once they learned that I lived in Exile they had called Dannon instead. Although he maintained good relations with the neighboring police departments and was a special friend of Chief Tate over in Bending Palms, cops all over the Panhandle knew better than to go near a citizen of Exile without first talking to Chief Dannon.

It is one of the benefits of living in a town this small, and I felt a lot better having Dannon with me as we headed over to meet the Davis investigators. Of course I had done nothing wrong, and meant to be completely forthcoming, but as a member of the Exile community I enjoyed the special paternal protection provided by Chief Dannon.

We rolled up outside the Davis police station, and

I noticed that it was the only station for miles around that had a second story on it. The Davis force was not all that big, and the policing in Davis was not all that involved, but the station was quite modern and I suspected they even had an actual detective or two on staff.

I was right about that, as the desk sergeant buzzed us through a security door and took us down a spotless corridor to an office which held three desks and three guys in plainclothes. I was surprised to see they were all young, early thirties at most, but they were neatly decked out in dress shirts and ties and they seemed polite enough as they stepped up to shake hands.

The first, a handsome sport with a deep tan, had been in several pictures from the drug bust at the Seaview. He was the only one wearing a shoulder holster, and seemed slightly amused as he shook my hand and thanked me for coming down.

"Hank Spears, Mr. Cole, Davis police force. This is Detective John Mayfair, and this is Detective Pete Ramirez." The other two both approached and shook my hand, greeting Chief Dannon as someone they had met many times before. Mayfair was tall and tan like Spears, and Ramirez looked like he could give Manny Batista a run for his money at arm wrestling.

They didn't go back to their desks, and I had to remind myself that a murder was an unusual event for them. Almost as unusual as a major drug bust.

"I saw you on the news the other morning. The drug bust at the Seaview," I offered to Spears.

"Yeah, well, it never rains but it pours, you know? Most of the time we're just backup for the street patrol, but every now and then things get interesting."

"Must be a full moon," added Ramirez brightly.

I was just beginning to wonder where all this was going when Dannon spoke.

"I'll be sitting in on this, if it's all right." He dropped the park ranger hat on one of the desks and grabbed a spare chair, and I had to admire the way he asked to be allowed to stay by telling them that was exactly what he was going to do.

Their reaction was peculiar, but I now saw that the three Davis detectives had been waiting for Dannon to leave. Three uniform smirks broke out on their faces, and Spears spoke for the group.

"Why, that would be fine, Chief. We're all friends here." He turned to take a seat behind his desk, signaling for me to pull up one myself, and I saw that Dannon's presence was definitely not fine. I began to doubt if the Davis detectives and the police chief from Exile were friends.

I got a quick look around the room while Mayfair and Ramirez went back to their seats. The office was rectangular, probably fifteen by twenty-five, with the long wall facing the door. Mayfair was to the left, facing into the room, while the other two faced the door. Ramirez sat with his back to the long wall and the room's only window, a few feet behind Spears and to the right. The place was painted a light green, and I noted the absence of a bulletin board, whiteboard, or any other kind of wall decoration. All three desks displayed stand-up picture frames of wives and children, but apart from that they were surprisingly empty.

The Davis detective squad room, it seemed, was not a very busy place.

"Okay, Mr. Cole, we spoke at length with Mr. Corelli at the Midnight Taxi Service, so it seems you've been helping out a P.I. from Atlanta, a Curtis Winslow, who was trying to find Dennis Sharp. Is that correct?"

"Yes, it is." I wondered at the specific nature of this opening, having been taught by other interviewers, both lawyers and investigators, to let the subject do the talking.

"There are two other unidentified people who were looking for Mr. Sharp?"

"They gave me their names as Harry Ames and Mark Knight when I met them two nights ago. The desk clerk at the Seaview also spoke with them."

Spears turned and made eye contact with the other two. Both Mayfair and Ramirez were taking notes, and returned his look with knowing stares. He turned back to me with a slightly puckered mouth.

"How did they know he'd been at the Seaview?"

"I don't know about how those two found that out, but Winslow had gotten a tip from one of his firm's offices in another city. Say, have you called Winslow?" I wasn't sure just how much of Winslow's confidence I could reveal here, but I felt sure he didn't want any of the bogus credit card story getting out.

"We left a message with his office in Atlanta. His cell phone seems to be off." This came from Mayfair.

"He'll want to know that the kid is dead."

"Oh, I imagine so."

"It would probably end the missing person part of this," added Ramirez, giving me a nod while narrowing his eyes and squinching up his mouth. I could not tell if this was meant to be sarcastic or reassuring, so I guess you could say it failed to do either.

"These other two, Ames and Knight, they told you they were bounty hunters?"

"No. In fact, they went out of their way to say they weren't bounty hunters or bail agents or anything like that. They said they were trying to get in touch with the kid to suggest he go back and face the music in Mobile."

"That's strange," Spears stated flatly.

"Yeah, especially when the bond was posted down in Miami." That came out before I had a chance to really think about it, giving me a momentary impression that Spears was better at interviewing than I had at first thought. It only lasted the moment, though, as he started talking again and convinced me I was right the first time.

"No, I mean we have to consider those two as prime suspects in a murder, and yet they were concerned about being mistaken for bounty hunters. That doesn't fit."

"I'm an amateur here, so I hope this doesn't sound

crazy, but if you suspect them in the kid's murder, why were they looking for him after killing him?"

Spears was still thinking, but he didn't take offense at what I'd said. On the contrary, he looked like the Cheshire cat when he answered me.

"We're not sure they actually were looking for him, Frank. We think they might have been trying to establish just where he went between the time he left the Seaview and the time they caught up with him. Saying they were looking for him gives them a cover story while diverting suspicion at the same time."

"They did want to know if he was carrying anything when he flagged down Billy Lee."

"Really?" This seemed to be the first new information I had supplied, as Spears became slightly more animated and the other two looked up when they heard the words. "Anything in particular?"

"Yes, they tried to make it sound as if they were concerned he might be moving on, but they asked if he was carrying a bag or a suitcase."

Spears glanced at the other two, who seemed to indicate that this was important information without saying so. Coming back to me, Spears continued.

"Okay, Frank, sorry to do this to you, but we're going to have to ask you all the questions we asked Mr. Corelli, right from the start. We got a good general understanding from him, but you're the guy with the answers.

"So. Feel like helping us?"

WE GOT OUT OF THERE TWO hours later, and even though things stayed civil I was glad that Dannon didn't get called away. The Davis detectives were clearly focusing on the two phony bail bonds guys as their primary suspects, and the whole thing ended with a fascinating workup of two sketches based on my description of the two men.

Davis didn't have a sketch artist, but they had the computers for the task and I felt right at home. Even if I couldn't express what I had seen, they just kept switching features in and out, thinning a face here, lengthening the hair there, until I felt they had a pretty good rendition. They even gave me a copy before Dannon and I headed back to Exile.

"Chief, do you think those guys were telling me everything?" I asked after we had gotten a good distance from the station.

He had almost burst out laughing at my question. "I sure hope not, Frank. This is a murder investigation, after all, and you're really just an ancillary witness."

"That's not what I mean. They didn't seem interested at all when I told them that Dennis Sharp's motel room looked directly down on the drug guy's car."

"I'm sure they thought it was just a coincidence."

"The local police snag a carload full of drugs, a guy who seems to have been watching that car shows up dead, and it's just a coincidence?"

"You said it yourself, Frank, the night clerk gave him that room because he was afraid the kid would skip on him. Besides, the kid ran off as soon as the police showed up, and his record doesn't suggest anything heavy like that guy Baxter was into."

Ronald Baxter, the traveling salesman arrested at the motel, had proven a tough nut for the police to crack. Despite his genuine status as an office-supply guy roaming the region at will, he had refused to provide the police with any information at all. He was currently sitting in a nearby prison where the local district attorney was arguing with the federal government over whose case this was. This was all information that Dannon had wheedled out of the detectives with a few judicious questions rationed out one at a time, and I would have learned none of it if he hadn't been there.

"I'd been meaning to ask you about that. Based on what they found in the trunk, the number of police at the Seaview that night was justified. But when they first encountered Baxter it was over a car alarm that kept going off. He was nothing more than a frazzled salesman, and yet the footage showed half the Davis police force, including that detective."

We were into Bending Palms by then, and I figured Dannon was concentrating on his driving in the town's busy shopping district. He took a long time to answer, anyway.

"Yeah, well, I'm not going to make any excuses for the folks in the Davis P.D. You hit the nail on the head, Frank, and you're not the first. I was here in Bending Palms just yesterday for court, and two of the bailiffs began joking with me about that. The general consensus is that the Davis police got tipped off about that car, and it doesn't take too much imagination to guess one of them set off that car alarm to get Baxter to come out of his room."

The thought had occurred to me, but it hadn't matched up well with the cops' decision to take the car to an impound and search it. If they'd known what was secreted in the vehicle's innards, what would stop them from opening it up right there?

Dannon continued, "I'm just going off of what the bailiffs said here, but the heavy betting says they popped the trunk, didn't see anything right away, and got spooked. So they went back to following the rule book and hauled the thing away for a thorough going-over."

"You think this was the first time they ever bumped into one of these?" I asked, already pretty certain that Chief Dannon did not have a lot of respect for the Davis P.D.

"That's it exactly. I think they got a tip about that car, and those three hotshots got a little excited. They could have waited until he came out the next morning, caught him half-asleep and with his hands full of luggage, but instead they alerted him something was up. In this case he came outside to kill the car alarm and got nabbed, but it could have ended with a lot of shooting instead. Lucky for them he wasn't armed.

"Don't tell anybody I said this, Frank, but the police

over in Davis are long on money and short on horse sense. Not that we do much policing over in Exile, but I've trained my guys to keep their eyes and ears open. Most of what I've learned about life has come from just paying attention to the people and the things around me, and the Davis cops don't appear to do that. They're too busy looking at themselves in the mirror.

"Take that guy Spears, for example. Who wears a shoulder holster in this heat, except for somebody trying to look like a big city detective?"

He shook his head minutely.

"You have to be a little sympathetic, I guess, because of where they are. They're in a town run by rich people, and the attitude rubs off on them a little. In the meantime, most of their work boils down to making sure no one bothers the rich folks, so it's not surprising that they weren't ready for the real thing.

"So yeah, I'm sure they kept some things from you because this is a murder investigation, and yeah, I think they kept some things from both of us because this case might not bear up under the wrong kind of eyes."

"Is it really that bad? What could they have done that would jeopardize a case like this?"

"Nothing criminal, mind you, but probably something procedural that might get the whole thing thrown out of court if Baxter comes up with a big enough lawyer."

"I see." I turned that one over in my head a few times, still unwilling to let go of the coincidental location of the kid's room. "You mean, something like who tipped them off about the car?"

He didn't answer right away, but a ghostly smile appeared under the sunglasses as we rolled up outside my place.

"You know, Frank, you really need to drop that taxi gig and concentrate on the investigations side of things. You have a good head for it."

I got out, and waved as I started toward my porch. It was still quite hot out, even though the sun was starting to head for the horizon, and I was thinking about sitting out on my porch for a while before heading to work. Dannon called after me.

"Frank?"

"Yeah, Chief."

"Get a good meal inside you tonight, willya? For me?"

A warm wave passed over me. It was the first time he'd mentioned the weight loss, but he'd said it so that it didn't come across as an insult. For the thousandth time I thanked my lucky stars for dropping me in Exile instead of someplace bigger. Where else does the chief of police say something like that? I pointed a crooked finger at him as I replied.

"For you, sure."

FIVE

I KEPT MY PROMISE TO DANNON, and not just because the chief of the Exile police had asked me nicely. My appetite was returning, and it had started with the meal that Beth Ann had brought by the cabstand the night before. I'd even been sound asleep when Dannon had come by that afternoon.

The link between these two salubrious developments and the new case was not lost on me, even if I'd needed Beth Ann's healthy nudging to see the connection. Perhaps the extra work involved in the case required additional calories and real rest, or perhaps this was all related to the added stress of having a crime brought right to the bulletproof glass of the cabstand. Regardless of what was causing the uptick in my eating and sleeping habits, it was welcome.

I called Ruby on the radio after taking over the guard shack that night, having thought of something while eating dinner and needing his advice. He told me he would swing by sometime that night, and just after dark I saw the battered yellow Midnight van come down the quiet street. Ruby got out and walked easily toward the back door of the office, his exaggerated waddle of that morning forgotten.

"What's up, Frank? You got a bucket of water rigged up over the door?" he called from outside. I walked to the entrance and opened it myself to show it was safe, and he sat down in the chair which Winslow had occupied the previous evening. I had not heard from the Atlanta P.I. yet, although I had to believe he had contacted the Davis police by then. As much as P.I.'s do not like to discuss investigations with law enforcement, possible implication in a murder is good reason to be forthcoming.

"Rube, has anybody heard from Billy Lee? I was down at the Davis P.D. all afternoon and they haven't been able to find him anywhere. His mother won't tell them where he's gone." Corelli had told the other drivers that the kid had turned up dead, and so there was little need to impress the seriousness of the situation on Ruby.

"Tony's his best friend, and he hasn't heard word one." Ruby's permanent look of concern tightened a little when I looked at him questioningly. "Yeah, I asked him, even before we heard about that kid getting murdered. If Tony hears from Billy Lee he's going to tell me."

"The cops are looking for the two guys who came by here a couple of nights ago." I handed him a copy of the sketches. "This is what they looked like. Mrs. Lee hasn't seen anybody like that around her neighborhood, so maybe they don't know which driver gave the kid a lift yet."

He looked at the paper briefly and looked up, shaking his head.

"I haven't seen anybody like this, either, even though these two look pretty average. Like as not I'd miss them in a crowd unless they came right up and started talking to me."

"I don't think they'd do that, with what I told them the other night, so I got to thinking about how else they might figure out who gave the kid a lift. If I wanted to know which Midnight cab rolled by the Seaview that night, I'd stake the place out at about the same time for a few nights, see if one went by."

"That wouldn't work. Seaview's on a main drag, taxis going from Davis to P.C. all the time, they'd see all sorts of cabs, and Midnight cars, too. That wouldn't help."

"Still, they might be dumb enough to see you or one of the others roll by and decide to take a chance."

"That why you've been so antsy about us?"

"Partly. What do you think about my idea? Make any sense?"

"No offense, Frank, but there's just too many rigs on that route all day and all night for them to pick one out." He cocked his head to the side and thought about something, and then spoke. "So maybe they don't do what you'd do. If it was me, I'd wonder if that driver got nervous with all the people asking questions and maybe took a few days off, like Billy Lee did."

"I did tell them he was unavailable."

"Yeah. And so they might try to figure out who he is by finding out who isn't out on the road."

"Could somebody do that?"

"Well, the quickest way would be to flag down a Midnight car and try to get the driver talking about the hours, the shifts, who's baggin' it and how much extra work he has to do because we're shorthanded." He let that rebound around his head. "Yeah, that'd work, except our guys are on the lookout. So far nobody's been around asking.

"Next, they'd likely try to get the dispatcher to tell them, but they already blew it with you, and Corelli wouldn't give them what you gave them. So that's out."

He snapped his fingers.

"Here's how they might do it. They can't ask Midnight people because they're afraid you warned us. So they might go asking a couple of the other services, you know, get the competition talkin' bad about us."

"Think that would work? These guys seemed serious enough to do something like that."

"You know, the more I think about this the more I think it would. Drivers bump into each other all over, and Billy Lee is a conspicuous kind of guy. In fact, I know just who to ask." He held up the sketch. "Can I keep this? Show it around?"

"It's yours. I made enough copies for everybody."

"Give 'em to me." He stood up, hitching up his pants. I handed him a folder with enough prints for half the cabs in Davis, and he started for the door.

"Gimme an hour or so to touch base with the others, and probably a whole day after that to see if anybody's been tapping the competition for gossip." He looked down at the sketch. "Be nice to put these two behind bars. Killin' a man that young is just wrong, no matter what he did. No way for anybody to behave."

WINSLOW CALLED ME A LITTLE later, and I was more than a little relieved to hear from him. Although I was convinced of his authenticity and his dismay at being had, life as the Davis police department's expert on Dennis Sharp was getting awfully lonely without him.

"Hang on to your hat, cowboy," he announced cheerfully, and I heard the sounds of a busy airport around him. "I'm headed back down there. I'm gonna meet with the Davis P.D. tomorrow morning, and, man, have I got news."

"Can I go with you?" I blurted out. Eating a good meal seemed to have done a lot for my energy level, if not my self-restraint.

"Wouldn't do it without you, pardner. I'd be in some big mess right now if it weren't for you.

"Okay, here's the big news. The Sharps cut a deal with the government so I could talk to them, and the feds fell all over themselves to get me a conference call. The gloves are off for the Sharp family now that their kid is dead, and apparently they'd been sitting on some information about how some big money left the country just before they were caught. So they gave that up and I got to talk to them.

"When it became clear they were going inside, they arranged with the kid to leave taped messages at an answering service they could call up on the prison phones. That way, if the kid ran into trouble he could at least let them know what was happening.

"Apparently he did this almost a week ago, but their phone privileges didn't let them get at the message until the night the kid was at the Seaview. He told them that he had run afoul of this gang in Mobile, a bunch of tough nuts known as the Springers, and his way of paying them back was to pull a job for them. Apparently the Springers feel their turf runs pretty far down the Gulf Coast, and this other gang from Miami was starting to cut into their territory."

"Baxter and the drugs."

"Among other things, yes. Baxter had a perfect cover, being a real traveling salesman with no criminal record, but the Springers found out about him hauling contraband for their rivals and decided to put him out of business. They told the kid that he had to steal the car when Baxter was overnighting in Davis, which he routinely did, and so that's why the kid was there."

It fell into place nicely. The kid was a smooth operator, and had been waiting until the wee hours of the morning to cross the parking lot and steal the car. The drugs were hidden in the body of the car, so there was no way that Baxter could have moved them into his room with him. Besides, apparently he had no need to suspect any trouble.

Unfortunately, someone had tipped off the Davis cops, who had beaten Dennis Sharp to the punch. I briefly considered Denny Dannon's observation that the Davis police should have waited until the next morning to apprehend Baxter, and almost laughed into the phone. Just how would all those cops have reacted, upon observing a street kid trying to boost the car of the drug runner they were preparing to arrest?

"And he left that message for his parents?"

"Yep. The feds tell me these Springers are rough customers, so the kid was in deep trouble. He didn't expect to come out of this alive, from what his folks tell me, and was trying to establish his last known whereabouts for them. Probably expected the Springers to kill him even after he'd pulled off the job. Anyway, he gave them the alias he was using at the time—"

"Taylor."

"Exactly. That's why they gave me that name, knowing it was what he was traveling under at the time. Apparently the kid hasn't used the name Sharp in months."

"His prints were the only thing linking him to that name, the two times he was picked up and gave an alias."

"That's right. Nobody who met this guy in the last year or so would have known him as Dennis Sharp.

"Anyway, the mother accessed the tape and started greasing palms at the prison. That got her a few more phone calls, one to her husband and one to their lawyer, who called up my firm and engaged us on the phony missing person case. That's where the story of the family credit card came from. They had to be able to explain why they thought the kid was at the Seaview that night."

My mind was processing this information at a rapid pace. I had become immersed in the facts and the details to such an extent that it all began to line up for me. I asked the same question I'd asked Denny Dannon.

"So the big issue right now is who tipped off the police?"

"Very good. My money's on the Springers. They knew about the car and the intended robbery, and I bet they were setting the kid up to go away for a long time, driving a car full of drugs. No honor among thieves, Frank."

I quickly filled him in on my discussion with the Davis P.D. and Chief Dannon's suspicion that the Davis cops had jumped the gun. I left the chief's name out, so in a way I took credit for that bit of deduction.

"That's even better. And believe me, I'm gonna find out just what that tip was all about when we see those guys tomorrow."

"Curt, has your missing person case turned into a murder case?" It had occurred to me that Winslow's initial assignment was already concluded. Concluded sadly, but finished nonetheless.

"It has. Apparently the Sharps had a fair amount of money left over when they went inside, and my firm is now formally retained. Never thought I'd see the day, but then again I bet I'd be quite surprised if I actually knew the identities of some of the people I've worked for over the years.

"And yes, Frank, you're working this as a contract assistant if you want."

I didn't know how to respond to that, except to try to crawl through the phone line and shake his hand. I was mumbling my thanks and agreement when I absently swiveled the chair and came face-to-face with the little blonde teenage girl from Dennis Sharp's photo booth picture.

I SAID GOODBYE TO CURT and took the entire two steps required to cross the hut's small floor. It brought me right up to the figure beyond the glass, and it was definitely her. The bail guys had said the photo booth snapshot was more recent than the high school yearbook photo, but I still hadn't figured on the girl actually being in the area. I was still considering this when the girl, who had been looking about her nervously, finally spoke.

"Let me in, mister. I need to talk to you."

Later on, I had to question my decision to let her in. After all, there were two dangerous thugs out there who had visited the office once before, and who knew if she was with them or not? After all, how else would the dead kid's girlfriend know of his connection to the cabstand?

Of course the kid could have been headed to meet her when he flagged Billy Lee down that night, I supposed. I then experienced a fleeting mental picture of a still-living Dennis Sharp hopping out of Billy Lee's taxi at the Davis boardwalk and meeting his lady love somewhere in the crowd. Right after that I wished for the hundredth time that Billy Lee would get in touch with us, as I had no way of knowing what I might be letting into the booth.

It was the eyes that did it, though. The girl had lost the ringlet pigtails and had her hair pulled back in a ponytail, highlighting her face's most striking characteristic. Her eyes were the color of the deep sea on a sunny day, and she looked so young and frail and frightened that I found myself unlocking the door as if she were my own offspring. She was through the narrow opening like a cat rushing in from the rain.

It would not be the last time that I compared her to an animal, and I think that was the basis of her considerable allure. It was impossible to guess her age, as she could have been anywhere between fifteen and twenty. She was short and small, but the amount of flesh that I could see was taut without being muscular. She had on a tight set of cutoff jeans and a T-shirt tied to the side of her waist, exposing a flat midsection and a pierced navel.

She looked out the windows without turning away from me.

"Can people see in here?" she asked quickly, and if I had to put money down I would have said she was closer to fifteen than twenty, just based on her voice.

"Yes." If she had been watching the booth prior to

showing herself she would have known the answer to her own question, which suggested she had not spent any more time waiting to get in there than absolutely necessary. At any rate, my answer displeased her and she dropped down into a crouch so that she was not visible from the street.

It was such a lithe, practiced movement that it put a heavy punctuation mark on the impression of an animalistic existence. The way her eyes darted about while never quite losing sight of me, the grace with which she had appeared and then hidden herself—all said the girl was accustomed to being someone's prey.

I pointed a baffled finger at the chair which had hosted Ruby's expansive backside an hour before.

"You don't have to squat down like that. If you slouch down in that chair no one's going to see you."

She gave it a quick look and decided in an instant that it would suffice. Without rising above the level of the windows she glided over and reclined. I had meant for her to sit normally, just hunched over a bit, and her frank display of herself surprised me. The ratty threads of her cutoffs cut into the flesh of her thighs as she extended her legs, and I decided I'd gone as far down that road as I intended.

I sat down at the desk, half-turned away from her.

"What's your name, mister?" she asked.

"Frank Cole," I replied. "What's yours?"

"Sally. Sally Hayes." She stopped looking around for a second, and when I turned to look those blue eyes bored right into me, as if she were judging whether or not I was the kind of guy who should know her name. "You got any food, Frank?"

I did, actually, as my eyes had been larger than my shrunken stomach when I bought dinner. I opened the small fridge and took out half of a large submarine sandwich, what we up north would call a grinder, and stole one of Corelli's sodas. I was halfway through this effort before it occurred to me that I hadn't given it a conscious thought. Handing the food across, I looked into the eyes again and made a note to ask the next cop I met if runaways learn how to hypnotize people.

She unwrapped the sandwich quickly, gave it the merest inspection, and then wolfed it down in the space of ten seconds. She opened the soda can and washed it all down while continuing to fix me with those blue headlights. I waited for her to say something else.

"My boyfriend's missing, Frank, and the last thing I'm sure he did was take a Midnight cab somewhere three nights ago. I have to find him."

The words tumbled out in a rush.

I lost the vision of her meeting her boyfriend at the Davis boardwalk that night, as that meeting obviously never took place. Before I could get back to how she knew to come to the cabstand, she continued breathlessly.

"I have a picture of him—" she began, trying to accomplish the impossible act of tucking a hand into the pocket of her cutoffs.

I suppose the intelligent thing would have been to call the police and let them tell her that her boyfriend was no longer among the living, but I just couldn't let her go on like that. So I told her.

"Sally, the police came by asking the same question you are." I reached into my file and came up with the mug shot bulletin about the fugitive Dennis Sharp. I held it out to her, and asked gently, "Is this your boyfriend?"

"No. No." The second word came out as a low wail, like a small child who didn't want to go to bed. Her hand came away from her pocket and she reached out for the paper. Her voice went up a notch, and she asked in a rushed whisper, "Why do you have this?"

"I told you. The police came by. That is your boyfriend, isn't it?"

Her hands began trembling, and she turned off the blue laser beams for a moment so that she could look at the floor. The tears were rolling for real when she looked up again.

"He's dead, isn't he?"

"I'm sorry, but that's true." I was nodding at her ever so slightly, my face set in an expression of sympathy, when she simply leaned across the short distance between us and put her head on my shoulder. She was still clutching the bulletin in both hands, but her body was wracked with tears, and so I put my arms around her while making the shushing sound that most people use on crying babies.

The only thing that made me put an end to it was the possibility of Beth Ann screeching into the parking lot with a late snack for me. That, and the dead accuracy

Beth Ann had displayed at the pistol range during one of our early dates.

Bringing my hands to her shoulders, I slowly pressed her away and whispered, "They can see us from outside. Remember."

She nodded dully and receded into her chair. Her eyes were red, but I needed to know how she had come to the cabstand in the first place.

"Sally, how did you know your boyfriend took one of our cabs?"

She sniffed hard. "He called me. From a phone booth. He said he was coming to meet me, to be watching for a Midnight taxi cab."

I suppose that made sense. "Where was he supposed to meet you?"

"There's a spot down by Graner Beach, a lot of the kids hang out there, it's a safe place to meet...don't you guys keep records? Why wouldn't you know that?"

Graner Beach was actually one of the less popular stretches of sand in Davis, and I am told it is a place where you can buy illegal things from a constantly changing mob of young people.

"He didn't go to Graner," I replied, strangely eager to correct the misconception that I didn't know what was going on. "He was dropped off at the Davis boardwalk."

She considered that for a few heartbeats.

"Why would he go there? He was supposed to meet me at Graner."

"Was your boyfriend in some kind of trouble, Sally?"

"What did they do to him?" It was as if I hadn't spoken. "Did they hurt him bad?"

"No, the police said it was a single gunshot wound, very quick." I looked at the ground before continuing. "Who are they, Sally? Who is 'they'?"

That did it. A mask slid down over her face, and she could have been a statue for all I was going to get out of her after that. She gave the door a quick glance, judging the distance, and I decided to back off before she bolted completely.

"Listen, if you're in any kind of trouble, I can call the police right now and they'll protect you." I almost didn't continue, but it seemed like a good point to make, so I did. "They'd let you see your boyfriend one last time, too."

She was standing now, and despite her size I knew better than to try and stop her.

"Thanks for helping, Frank. That sandwich was good." She lifted the half-empty soda can. "Can I take this?"

"Sure. But wait." I turned and scribbled down my cell phone number on a dispatch slip. "Here's my number, if you change your mind about talking to the police."

She reached out for it with just the hint of an expression showing, something between suspicion and interest.

"That all you're giving me this for?" she whispered, and I saw with an earth-shattering clap of the obvious that I was not the first older guy to give her his number.

I began babbling that I didn't want anything from her, that it was just if she changed her mind, but she cut me off with a dim smile.

"That's okay, Frank, I can tell the good guys from the bad ones." She held my gaze as she went out the door, and even though I was completely befuddled, and she was juggling the soda and the police bulletin, I did notice that she managed to use the bulletin to turn the doorknob.

"OH, YOU BET SHE DIDN'T touch the doorknob!" laughed Winslow as we sped down the highway toward Davis. "From the sound of it, the only other thing she touched that could hold a fingerprint was that soda can, and she was smart enough not to finish it."

"So what do you make of it?" I asked, trying not to show my annoyance at his merriment. He had picked me up at my house in Exile that morning, and had been astounded that I let her in the dispatch hut at all. He had then told me some gruesome stories from his years as a Detroit cop, tales of seemingly defenseless street people who had done great harm to unsuspecting victims. I sincerely hope he was exaggerating, embellishing the details in an effort to get me to be more careful.

"Well, this whole case is so jumbled up that I'm not ruling anything out just yet, but I have to wonder if that fingerprint habit was just something she picked up from her old boyfriend Dennis. Remember that was the only thing that consistently tripped him up, and from the sound of things our little lady friend doesn't want the same thing happening to her."

I had gone back online after coming off shift earlier, and there was absolutely no record of a Sally Hayes in any of the criminal databases I had searched. She didn't turn up in the runaway listings, either, and with nothing more than a possibly phony name to go on, there was little else I could do.

"But our friend Dennis didn't mention her in his message to his parents, so she's a definite wild card. And Frank—" He took his eyes off of the road to look at me. "When we see the police, no mention of the girl, all right?"

"Why not?"

"Because I think you're right that they were holding out on you, and I don't want to bring these guys in on every detail of our case. I want them focused on the most important thing, which is finding Billy Lee." He shook his head. "And I still can't believe they haven't found him yet. His mom knows he's hiding out, he has almost no money, it's a textbook fugitive situation."

Winslow was wearing a dark business suit, and his rental car was an expensive town car this time. It was not a stretch to believe he had dressed formally for his meeting with the police, but the whole ensemble suggested he was in no mood to accept abuse from the Davis cops.

"So why do you think they haven't found him yet?"

"Truthfully, I believe they aren't really looking. That

story you told me about the car alarm and all the cops at the scene stinks to high heaven, and I bet these guys wish this dead kid was never found. What they want right now is for that drug case to go to court with no more questions asked and no connection to this dead con man."

"And we're about to go in there and show them the connection."

"Big time."

THE INTERVIEW DID NOT GO quite as long as mine had the day before. Detective Spears started the show, and Winslow ran him over as if he were still behind the wheel of the town car.

"So, Frank, why didn't you tell us you were actually working with Mr. Winslow here?" the senior detective asked before we were fully through the door to the detectives' office. Pete Ramirez and John Mayfair were with Spears.

"Frank did the initial background checking on his own, in response to a threatening visit directly related to his night job at the cabstand. I offered to purchase that information and pay for his time when I saw that he was the only person—law enforcement or otherwise—who made the connection between the drug bust at the Seaview and Dennis Sharp.

"Now deceased." He sounded like a lawyer, but he swung a leg up and over the back of one of the office chairs and plopped himself down like a patron at a lunch counter. He leaned forward, dropping his fingertips onto Spears's desk with a thud. "Now how about we all sit down like adults and hash this thing out to our mutual satisfaction?"

My P.I. friends have a general response to the police, which is to treat them politely and tell them nothing, so Winslow's behavior was outlandish in the extreme. I half expected Spears to start threatening to arrest us both, but clearly something Winslow had said struck a chord. Spears smiled at the big man, now seated, and waved an open palm at another seat for me.

"Sure, Mr. Winslow. Let's start the hashing by talking about your clients. What makes you think we should believe anything that two lifelong grifters say? Particularly two who are convicted felons doing hard time."

"Because their kid is dead."

"All the more reason to suspect whatever they told you. You ever hear of revenge? You know who the Sharps have defrauded over the years?" He pointed in the direction of a closed brown file on his otherwise empty desk. "Some pretty heavy people. People who might decide to get even by going after their family members. Ever think of that?"

"Sure. Except no one knew the kid was dead when my firm was retained." I didn't know how much Winslow had told Spears about the fraudulent missing person case which had set him on Dennis Sharp's trail, and from the way Winslow was talking I believed he might have left that part out.

"So they just happened to retain you a day before the murder?"

"The Springers."

"What?"

"The Springers. You seemed familiar with them when we talked on the phone. The Sharps say the Springers put their son up to stealing the car carrying the drugs, the one you busted just before he fled the motel."

Spears swallowed with as little fanfare as possible, and Ramirez jumped in to save him.

"So they say. Once again, it's two convicted confidence people telling a story. Me, I think there's no connection at all."

Winslow turned his head slowly and stared at the Davis detective.

"Works for me. Whaddya say I head over to Mobile and talk with some of these Springer people? They deny any knowledge of the kid, and we're done here."

I almost fell off my chair. I knew next to nothing about this gang in Mobile, but from what Winslow had told me they were pretty rough. The very idea of trying to contact that kind of person was totally beyond me, and here was Winslow talking about calling them up for a meeting as if they worked in the same office building.

"You think the Springers are gonna talk to you? More than likely cut your—" Ramirez was standing up now, his voice rising. Something in Winslow's expression must have set him off, most likely another cop-to-cop thing of which I was ignorant.

"Hold on, Pete, hold on." Spears raised his hand, and Ramirez stopped his forward movement. To Spears's left, John Mayfair—who had said nothing to this point—suddenly took his eyes off of Winslow and put them on Spears with a look of alarm. Spears, having stopped Ramirez, resumed speaking.

"Okay, Mr. Winslow. Go on over to Mobile. Talk to the Springers. You seem like a guy who'll listen to whatever line they'll give you. If they talk to you at all."

"Thanks for your time," Winslow said brightly, doing a reverse of the leg swinging action as he stood up. He almost kicked me in the head, but the movement was good enough to accomplish what he intended.

"Hold on, hold on." Spears was on his feet now, the tough guy act gone. I had no idea what was going on at this point, but I could see his bluff had been called and he wasn't ready for it. "Listen, let's you and me take a walk, and I'll try to fill you in on a couple of things."

"Don't do it, Hank," intoned Mayfair, now on his feet like Ramirez. As the only one still seated, I started to rise, but Spears jabbed a finger at me.

"Siddown. I'm only going to talk to Mr. Winslow here."

There was a lot of confrontational air in that small room, or maybe I'd been around Winslow too much, but I continued to rise. I stared at Spears with all the re-sentment I could muster, and found it was genuine. I'd been as nice as pie not even a full day before, and he'd just told me to sit down as if I were wearing handcuffs.

"That's okay, Detective." Winslow spoke slowly, starting to ease off on the accelerator. He took his keys from his pocket and went to give them to me, half turning away from the others. Winslow winked with the eye they couldn't see, and handed me the key ring. "Frank, how about you go make that phone call now? Tell 'em there's no need to go to Mobile after all. I'll call you when I'm done here."

I had the sense to play along, but I was out in his car, driving around Davis looking for a coffee shop, when I saw what Winslow had done for me. Maybe he did go for a walk with Spears, in which case I would have been left sitting in the main lobby for goodness knows how long. He'd let me out of there to save me face, but at the same time letting the Davis cops know that he could still call on someone to go visit the Springer gang of Mobile, Alabama.

I had to suspect there would be no need for a walk outside, though, now that I was out of earshot. In a way the roles were now reversed, and the police were the ones who wanted to share information with the private investigators. No matter what was happening back there, it looked like someone in this case was finally going to come clean.

SIX

"NAH, HE DIDN'T TELL ME everything, but then again I don't think he can." Winslow was driving again. He'd become intrigued by the coffee shop I'd visited, and while it was the last place I wanted to go, that's where we were headed. "Here's what makes me think that: The tip came from the Springers."

"He told you that?"

"Yes, he did. He didn't name the informant, but he said it was someone who wouldn't do that without the leaders knowing it."

"How could he say something like that?"

"Well, the Springers aren't your average gang, Frank. I had my people make some phone calls while I was working out a deal with the Sharps' lawyer, and they gave me a nice little workup. Seems the Springer gang gets its name from the main family in a nice, tight-knit group of relatives. There's almost a hundred of them, and to be anyone in that gang you have to be related."

"Kind of like the old Mafia."

"Oh, the Mafia's still like that, Frank, it's just they're so fragmented that it doesn't work very well anymore. Now, the Springers, they actually visit the new members in the maternity ward, so it's possible that Spears is right about this."

"But why would they tell Dennis Sharp to steal the car when they were going to tip off the cops?"

"That's the million-dollar question, and that's why the Davis cops believe that Mommy and Daddy Sharp are feeding me a line of nonsense. Except they're not thinking it through.

"Me, I believe the Sharps' story, if only because their kid is dead. So let's say they are telling the truth, and that Dennis was supposed to steal that car for the Springers. Now add in the cops' story, which I also believe to be true, that the Springers tipped them off about the car. Sounds like the Springers wanted to kill two birds with one stone, sending a message to their rivals that the Panhandle is theirs and not to move drugs through anymore, as well as getting Dennis Sharp apprehended at the wheel of a drug smuggling car. With his record that's maybe twenty years."

"But the cops took the car before the kid could steal it."

"Exactly. They jumped the gun, and poor Dennis ran out the side door looking for a phone booth to call his new bosses and tell them it didn't work."

"Who didn't believe him, and so they killed him."

"There's a good chance that's what happened. But the only question right now is why don't the Davis cops believe that?"

"Are they protecting the Springers? Now that they got a tip from them? Maybe to use them later?"

"I doubt that. If that guy Baxter hadn't used Davis as an overnight every time he rolled through, the Davis cops and the Springers would never even have met. No, I still think there's more to that car alarm story than they're telling us."

"You think they set the alarm off to get Baxter to come outside and they're worried about that affecting the court case?"

"No, it's bigger than that."

"How do you know?"

"Because Spears admitted that's what they did. And he would never have done that if there wasn't more to it."

"ANYWAY, I DID GET SPEARS to agree to get that sketch of yours out to the antigang people in Mobile, maybe see if your two bail guys are hired help for the Springers." Winslow settled in behind a plate of bacon and eggs, and I realized he hadn't eaten all day.

"You mean, they didn't send it out already?"

"That's right. Like I said, they aren't too keen to have their big drug bust looked at too closely. If I hadn't talked to them, they'd have slowly eased Dennis Sharp into the 'Unsolved' file after making it look like they gave it the old college try." He was making short work of his breakfast. "It sure would be nice to know who those two knuckleheads were, though."

"You think they did it? I gotta tell you, they didn't seem the type. They were more like a comedy act than a couple of hired guns."

"You'd be surprised. When I was a rookie patrolman, I guarded a hit man for the Detroit mob in between interrogations. He had the greatest sense of humor. Had me in stitches the whole time." He smiled at the memory. "The desk sergeant finally heard me laughing and pulled me out of there. I thought I was going to be walking foot patrol for the rest of my life.

"Anyway, it's a good job for Spears and his guys while we figure out where your friend Billy Lee is hiding."

I CALLED TONY NG ON HIS cell phone, and he joined us in a municipal park near Davis center an hour later. The sun was high in the sky, and Winslow had shed his jacket and tie while waiting. I was wearing a light collared shirt and a pair of khakis, but sweat ran down my arms as we waited.

"You ever gonna acclimate, Frank?" Tony sang out as he walked up. He had pulled his rig right up onto the grass a few yards away, protected by some strange cabbie god from getting so much as a citation. "If you were from Vietnam, you'd think this was a nice winter day."

"You were born about ten blocks from here, Tony."

"It's in the genes. Besides, I grew up in this kind of weather, and in case you haven't noticed, it's hotter than heck." He stuck his hand across the worn picnic table to greet Winslow. "Hi, Mr. Winslow. Tony Ng. Frank said you're trying to straighten everything out for Billy Lee."

"Billy Lee could straighten everything out himself if he'd just make a phone call."

"That so? Well, I'm one of his best friends and I have no idea where he went, so it must be pretty serious."

"Any idea what spooked him?"

"Two guys asking questions, is what I heard."

"That's what I mean. What did he think they were looking for?"

"I really don't know the answer to that one, except that the Lees are dirt poor and I think his old man got hassled by the IRS a time or two. Kind of upbringing where you answer the front door by runnin' out the back."

Winslow gave me a doubtful look, clearly not enjoying Tony's sense of humor. I was about to try and help when Tony dropped the routine.

"You guys think of talking to his last fare? The one he was hauling when Frank called?"

Winslow and I stared at each other.

"He had a passenger when Frank called him?"

"Yes, he did," I jumped in, getting a sinking feeling that normally accompanied an oversight on my part. "I told you that. At least I think I did. Didn't I?"

"No." He looked at Tony, who was now enjoying the show and his newfound importance. "You think he might have called somebody after he got off the phone with Frank?"

"Sure do. He dropped out of sight right after talking with Frank, so he probably called somebody while he was dropping off the last passenger." He shook his head, grinning. "Billy Lee never paid any mind to the folks in the backseat. No conversation, and if he was on his cell phone forget about getting his attention. That's why the corporate types always asked for him."

"Frank, any way we can figure out who that last passenger was?"

"Sure," I answered, kicking myself over and over. So many people had been asking about the record of Billy Lee's travels on the night of the drug bust, and here I had a possible source in that same computer, just on a different day. "Care to see the cabstand again?"

CORELLI'S IDIOT NEPHEW Jeff was on duty when we went by. I am not being uncharitable by calling him that, as it is a direct quotation from the idiot nephew's uncle. Corelli disliked leaving Jeff in charge of the office, and had hired me mainly as an excuse to cut down Jeff's hours.

Although I appreciated the odd night that Jeff took over the dispatch duties for me, he always horsed up the paperwork so badly that it usually took me two days to straighten things out. This time I was pleased to see him, because Corelli didn't like my switching nights with Jeff and I knew I was going to be busy most of the evening.

After securing Jeff's hearty thanks at the extra hours, I logged into the system and finally caught a break. Billy Lee's last fare had not been going to some non-specific place like the boardwalk or the beach. Instead, he had just finished an evening of bowling and headed straight home. A quick reverse address lookup on the internet gave us his name, and a quick search using his name showed that he worked at a computer store in Davis.

"Looks like we're going back to the park," I told Winslow as we headed back to the car.

Tim Sellers was in his early twenties, a bright young man who saw a good chance to peddle some business software when we walked into the small store near the center of town.

He was tall and thin, and with the addition of twenty years and a pair of plastic glasses he could have been Roger Canfield, the manager at the Seaview Motel. He showed more enthusiasm for his job than Roger did, though, coming out from behind the gray plastic polymer of the store's main desk to greet us.

The place was set up to appear very modern, which is a plus when selling computer equipment. The floor was carpeted, the walls were sided with the same textured gray plastic material as the desk, and an X-shaped cubicle displayed four computers in the center of the store. The walls were lined with flashy software boxes and broken out into business, personal, tax, and games, as advertised by large red stylized letters attached to the walls.

"Well, hello there, I'm Tim, welcome to our store. You two look like a couple of entrepreneurs looking for some software to help with the business." He wore the store's regulation gray shirt, complete with a white plastic nametag, but aside from the uniform he struck me as a guy who knew what he was doing. Winslow and I were both, in a way, entrepreneurs. Winslow might be employed by a large firm, but he had the air of a man who worked by himself most of the time and had no difficulties getting started on a job. As for me, I liked to think I was still an entrepreneur regardless of how my first venture had turned out.

"That's pretty close." Winslow was friendly without encouraging the man. "We're actually private investigators, and if we weren't here on official business we'd probably be here outfitting our office."

I kept a straight face and nodded intermittently at Winslow's introduction. I guess I could be lumped in as a private investigator because I was now drawing pay from Winslow's firm, but I did think that the part about buying things for our office was stretching it a bit.

"Private investigations? Here? In Davis?" He caught himself and actually looked toward the door before continuing with a lowered voice. "Are you tailing somebody?"

"Not exactly. But we are looking for someone, and we think you might be able to help us."

"Me? What, you think somebody you're looking for came in here? I mean, we've got some neat anti-hacking stuff but that's about the extent—"

"Actually, the man we're looking for gave you a ride from the Davis Lanes bowling alley to your home four nights ago." I stepped forward officially and held up Billy Lee's employment photo, borrowed from his personnel record at the office a half hour before.

"I know him. That's Billy Lee. But he's been around here forever, he's just a taxi driver—" Tim's face clouded over and his mouth hung open just a hair. I was afraid he was going to make the same assumption that Billy Lee had made, that the people asking the questions were creditors or worse, but he was on a completely different track. "You don't think he's a spy, do you?"

"Sir?"

This was a day of firsts. My first private investigations buff and my first view of a completely dumbfounded Curt Winslow.

"It all fits! What better cover than a taxi driver? Nobody notices you, you can go anywhere. Why, they park right on the grass in the park over there and no one gives them a ticket. Is that it?"

"Umm…no, not exactly—"

"Do you carry a gun?"

"No."

"Why not?"

"Because I might be tempted to shoot someone."

The kid wasn't sure what Winslow meant by that. I'm not sure what he meant by that, even now, but he sure sounded menacing. At any rate, it was lost on Tim, who then opened his mouth as if to yawn while pointing a bouncing finger at Winslow.

"Good one! That was a good one! 'I might be tempted to shoot somebody'—outstanding!" He laughed for just a moment, and then brought himself back under control. "So what do you want to know?"

"Mr. Sellers, we're just trying to find Billy Lee to ask him about another fare from a different night. Now, when you were being driven home from the bowling alley—"

"We qualified for the league tournament that night."

"Congratulations. Now, in the course of that ride we have reason to believe that Billy Lee received a cell phone call—"

"Did he ever. He was really mad at this one guy, I didn't catch much of it."

My ears began to burn.

"We have a pretty good idea what that conversation was about, but we're more interested in the second conversation."

"I did hear more of that one. He was talking to someone named Miranda."

I had the notebook out and was writing without being told.

"Did you hear what he said to Miranda?"

"Not really, I'm not rude—"

"I'm sure you're not."

"So far everyone we've interviewed has said that Billy Lee was a very loud talker," I threw in, and Tim's face relaxed.

"You know, he really is. Good guy, but loud. Anyway, yeah, I did hear some of it. He was talking to Miranda about an hourly rate, complained about his sunburn, said he'd see her later that night. That's about it."

Winslow was smiling now, even though I thought the name of Billy Lee's girlfriend was slim stuff to go on. He plucked a card from his jacket pocket and handed it to Tim.

"Tim, you've been very helpful. If you think of anything else would you mind calling us? That's my private number on the card."

Tim stared at the card like a winning lottery ticket.

OUTSIDE, I WANTED TO SHOW that I could do more than take notes, particularly after being shown up by Tony Ng on something as basic as questioning Billy Lee's last fare the night he disappeared.

"So you think this Miranda is Billy Lee's girlfriend? Maybe we should go talk to the cabbies again?" Guys who have no money and are also hiding out usually have to bunk down with someone they know, and the girlfriend is normally first on the list. I figured the other drivers might know something about Miranda, such as her address or last name, once we jogged their memories.

"Oh, I don't think so, Frank. Let's go down to the docks instead."

"You think Miranda is a stevedore?"

"No, I think Miranda is a boat. We're looking for a guy with no money who's supporting his mother. He needs a place to hide, but he also needs to keep bringing home the bacon. He was complaining about how easily he gets sunburned and wanting a better hourly wage, and whoever he was talking to was going to put him up for the night. Finally, no one has been able to find this guy, which suggests he may even have skipped town."

"You lost me."

"I'm sorry, Frank, thinking out loud. I think Billy Lee is moonlighting as a deckhand on some charter fishing boat or something like it. He keeps getting paid, he sleeps on the boat, and twelve to fourteen hours a day he's not in town." He opened the car door and looked at me over the roof of the car. "Your Billy Lee isn't as dumb as he acts."

MY MAGIC WITH DATABASES failed us completely at this point, as I know nothing about boats or how to track them down. Luckily Winslow had been doing this kind of work for long enough to know what to do, and I listened to his magic on the phone. He changed right before my eyes from a no-nonsense private investigator into a hick tourist, trying to run down a very fun charter boat he'd been on the year before.

"Yes, I think the name was *Miranda* but it might have been longer than that. You know, *Miranda's Horizon* or something like that. *Lady Miranda*…no, it wasn't a big-time cruise, pretty low-rent really, but it was right around here somewhere…yeah, some of the guys did a little fishing off the back end, but I can't say it was actually a fishing charter…" His voice trailed off as the travel agent on the other end began looking for a boat matching this free-form description.

"Bingo." He turned to me and gave the thumbs-up sign. "That's it. What was the name of the skipper, Captain Lou or something like that?" A pause and a grimace. "Well, I wasn't even close, was I? Was I at least right about them being around here?" Another pause and a wide grin. "There you go, I knew it. Thanks a lot…no, no, thank you, I'll book it myself."

He ended the call and turned the smile at me.

"So, night dispatcher, you know where Pier Two is in this town?"

THE BOAT'S NAME ACTUALLY was *Miranda,* with nothing before or after it, and it pulled in just before the sun went down. Pier One and Pier Two were located in a touristy part of Davis, a place where people went to take three-hour Gulf cruises, charter fishing trips, and snorkeling excursions. The two piers were surrounded by a variety of restaurants, mostly seafood places, as well as a number of T-shirt and souvenir shops. It was actually a fun place to go, and I had been there before.

I had never paid much attention to the returning charters, though, and they turned out to be a treat. Most of them were expensive fiberglass boats festooned with flying bridges, radio antennae, and folded outriggers, but there were a couple of wooden jobs as well. From the looks of the departing passengers, it had been a good day on the water.

Winslow and I were seated on a park bench near a giant rusting anchor, watching the vessels return. A deckhand seemed excited by a series of pennants flapping on a line at the back of his craft, and began pointing them out to the crew of the next boat over. They seemed to be nothing more than triangular nylon swatches bearing the silhouettes of unknown varieties of fish, but the next boat did not seem to have any.

"What're those?" I asked.

"Catch flags. They put one up for every fish they caught today, and they leave them up overnight. People thinking about taking a charter supposedly come down and see which boat has the most flags and ask to go out on that one the next day. Least that's the way they did it in the Bahamas when I went out last year."

Although the sun was setting, casting a shadow on the activity at the docks, it was still as hot as an oven. Winslow had shed his jacket and dress shirt for a lime guayabera, and had donned a light brimmed hat from the trunk of the town car. With the dark glasses on he looked like a retiree watching the sun go down, and I looked like an undernourished bum sitting nearby.

"Here we are," he announced pleasantly, as a wooden boat made a neat turn inside the space between the two piers and touched up to the dock nicely. Its white stern was facing us, and the name "Miranda" stood out in red letters. The *Miranda* looked more like a New England lobster boat than a deep-sea fishing vessel, but several catch flags fluttered in the evening breeze and a nuclear family of four was busily snapping pictures in the back.

That would have been nice enough, but the best thing was the sight of Billy Lee, his face and arms burned a fierce red, hopping nimbly to the dock and beginning to tie up. He wore sunglasses and a floppy fisherman's hat, but it was him.

"The guy tying up is Billy Lee."

"You wanna do this, or should I?"

"Let me talk to him." I stood up, smelling the salt air and stretching while the charter family got off the boat. They sure were happy about something, and there was a general discussion about visiting a T-shirt shop nearby for some commemoratives of their trip as they went by. By that time Billy Lee had finished tying up and was back aboard, opening a faded red plastic cooler and pulling out what appeared to be some kind of bait fish. He started cutting it up on a narrow wooden table built into the side of the boat, using a long, slender blade that looked like it could cut a steel cable in half.

I walked down the gently rocking dock until I was

directly across from him. His back was turned to me, and he was flipping the guts of the fish over the side where a group of gulls were hanging a few feet in the air. As the fish leavings flipped through the air, the birds swooped in with a series of screeches, fighting for the scraps. I cleared my throat.

"Billy Lee."

He turned slowly, still holding the knife, but when he recognized me his face broke into a grin.

"Frank! How ya doin', man?" He looked about him furtively, but without much urgency. "How'd you find me?"

"Long story, Billy Lee." He didn't seem mad at me anymore, so I decided to play a hunch. "You feel like comin' back to the cabstand?"

"Do I? You bet!" He looked toward the wooden wheelhouse and lowered his voice. "Man, this is hard work, Frank! Look at me! Probably getting' skin cancer even as we speak! And the skipper makes Corelli look like—"

I didn't get to hear the rest, as the skipper poked a red, peeling face out of the wheelhouse and told Billy Lee to get back to work or he wasn't getting paid. The guy looked to be a hundred years old and four feet tall, but when he opened his mouth, even I jumped.

Billy Lee pursed his lips, lifted his chin, and looked skyward, all with his face pointed away from the wheelhouse.

"Yessir, Cap'n. Whatever you say," he called out, and

the angry face disappeared. "Frank, I'm gonna be here an hour or so. Why don't you meet me at Tortoise Shell over there?" He pointed toward a seedy bar tucked in between a restaurant and a gift shop.

I nodded and started walking away, but he called after me in a near whisper. I turned to see the face of a man badly in need of rescue.

"You sure I can come back? Those fellas stop comin' around?"

"Yes to both."

He smiled and went back to the bait.

I walked up the dock to Winslow and pointed out the Tortoise Shell, with no real desire to go in and wait for an hour.

"Oh, I don't think so, Frank. Have a seat. This here's a little trick I learned about people who've already run off once before. You and I are going to watch Billy Lee until he actually walks right up to us."

WE DID GO INTO THE TORTOISE Shell, and it wasn't half as bad as it looked. First, the nuclear family was in there along with other tourists and I just couldn't believe the place was all that dangerous with clientele like that. Second, it was more of a no-frills diner than a waterside bar and I got a great big hunk of fish covered in lemon juice. Finally, Billy Lee was so fed up with life on the water that he was able to overcome his paranoia and talk to the total stranger with me.

"You just wouldn't believe how many times you have

to replace the bait," he complained, drinking beer from a mug and eating a burger that Winslow had bought for him. "I did this job once before, but I just plain forgot what a backbreaker it is. There's never a chance to just sit down, and just when you think the lines are set and all we have to do is cruise, old skipper there is telling me to reel it in and replace the bait."

I kicked him under the table, and when he looked at me I motioned behind him with my head. The nuclear family was trying to get his attention, and when he looked, they all grabbed pinches of their new T-shirts to show him the various fish images emblazoned on them. I supposed the individual selections represented their actual catches that day, but it had a bad effect on Billy Lee.

"I am never leaving that cab again," he said, swinging back around after waving in a friendly fashion at the day's happy passengers.

"Well, let's talk about that. The night you picked up the kid, it took twenty-five minutes for you to go just a few blocks. How'd that happen?" Winslow asked evenly, still careful of Billy Lee's skittish nature.

"Hey, Corelli just wants the start point and the end point recorded, he doesn't care if we go all over town."

"I get it. So did you take the kid somewhere along the way?"

"Sure, and that was the weird part. He asked to go out of town, to this abandoned weigh station on the highway near Bending Palms. I figured he was going to try and stiff me, but when I told him there was nothing out there he handed me a twenty like it was a five-cent coupon for prune juice.

"And that was the tip on a twelve-dollar fare. He knew exactly what I was really askin', that I was afraid he'd try to skip. Anyway, I took him out there and he went over to this really old pay phone. I told him it didn't work, but he went anyway. He wasn't gone but a minute, but when he came back he was different."

"Different how?"

"Like a guy who's just been told he's got a week to live. He sat down in back, and I asked him where to, and he asked me to give him a minute, like he was trying to get his thoughts together.

"He asked me if I had a map of the area, and I had a stack of those maps Corelli had printed—"

"The ones with the Midnight cab logo on them. That's how the Davis police connected him to us. They found one in his pocket," I explained to Billy Lee.

"Must be the one I gave him. He looked at it for a minute, and all of a sudden he came to and asked me to take him to the boardwalk in Davis. I took him there, told him it was twelve dollars, and he came up with another twenty. Told me to keep the change, forget I ever saw him, and I said, 'Saw who?' and he was gone."

"Was he carrying anything when he flagged you down?"

"No. Looked like any other college kid out on the town."

"Did he pick anything up at that phone booth?"

"It's not really a booth, it was one of those stand-alones, the kind with a backboard, two side flaps, and that's it. But yeah, he must've picked something up there, a message or something, but he wasn't carrying anything when he came back."

Winslow looked at me as if asking if I had anything to add, and I shook my head slightly. Obviously the kid had gone to a message drop at that pay phone, and he hadn't liked whatever had been left for him. Assuming he was supposed to have driven the stolen drug car there, perhaps the message had directed him to take the car somewhere else and he was trying to decide what to do next.

"Well, weird or not, for that kind of money he can ride in my cab anytime," announced Billy Lee as he finished off his dinner. He caught the startled look that Winslow and I gave each other. We'd been in such a hurry to ask questions that we'd completely forgotten to tell him that the kid was no longer among the living.

"I say somethin' wrong here?" he asked.

"WELL, THIS ISN'T MAKING a lot of sense to me," I told Winslow after we had dropped Billy Lee at his mother's house. It was well after dark, but I wasn't feeling sleepy even though I'd been on the go for over twenty-four hours.

"What's not making sense? The kid was supposed to steal the car and go to that weigh station to get instructions on where to take it. The Davis police messed that up, so he went to the weigh station anyway. He read the message, didn't like the idea of going wherever it said to go, and decided to run for it.

"He went to the boardwalk so he'd be harder to track, just in case Billy Lee met somebody else with a few twenties to spare. He doubled back to his little campsite to get his belongings, but somebody was waiting for him. That somebody killed him, and I think when we identify those two phony bail bondsmen we're gonna find out they work for the Springers, and that they're the ones who killed the kid."

"He gave Billy Lee forty dollars for cab fare, but he used a stolen credit card for a motel room that only cost forty-five dollars."

"He's a street kid, he knew he could talk his way around that night clerk, so why blow money on the room?"

"Exactly. Why get a room at all? Why take the chance that the real manager would notice the problem with the credit card? The night clerk said he was suspicious of the kid, so why invite that kind of attention?"

"You don't know people like this, Frank. With a grifter, half the motivation is the need to pull the wool over other people's eyes. The money's nice, but tricking people is the real thrill and they become addicted to it. Most of these jokers can't turn it off even when they know they should, which is why so many of them end up behind bars or under buildings. They take stupid chances when they don't need to."

I turned that over in my mind, recognized what was right about it, and decided where I wanted to go.

"You know, I think you're right. I don't know these people, and I don't know this kid. In fact, that's all he is to me, that's all he's ever been. The kid. The con man. Dennis Taylor. Dennis Sharp. The dead guy. What do we really know about him?"

"How long since you slept, Frank?"

"Not long enough, obviously. No, hear me out. We have a kid who's a rotten con man, has gotten caught all over the Gulf area, and the only reason he's not behind bars is because he can spin a story. Now, does that really fit? Can't get out of his own way, commits petty crimes in numerous states, but in the lockup he becomes an Academy Award winner."

"It's in the genes, Frank. Remember his parents."

"Yeah, let's remember his parents. The kid is twenty-four years old and they never taught him anything? Like not renting a room in the motel where you're going to steal a car loaded with drugs? If he's such an ace street person, why would he even need that room? The car was visible from the street, there's plenty of nooks and crannies to hide in around there, and yet he's perched directly across from his target. It doesn't add up."

"Well, which is it, Frank? Is he a master criminal who can talk his way out of a holding cell, or is he a knucklehead who rents a room in the same motel as his intended victim? You're what's not making sense." For the first time Winslow sounded as if he were tiring of my company.

"I'll tell you what. I had my office start digging into the kid's record in depth when I was talking to the parents. I didn't get a chance to sort through it, and now I don't feel I have to, but if you want I'll let you borrow it for the evening. There's really not that much, but you've been a sport and we'll just chalk it up to a little more background research. How's that sound?"

It sounded like a parting gift, a way to explain a small bonus before cutting me loose. As far as Winslow was concerned, the two bail guys were the most likely suspects, and now that their pictures were out it was just a matter of time before they were identified. He'd already run down the one loose end, which was Billy Lee, and found that the thread was meaningless. That left the two guys who had been searching for the kid they supposedly had killed, and that was good enough for him.

"That'd be great, thanks."

SEVEN

WE STOPPED BY WINSLOW'S motel so he could organize the documents and print off some related emails from his people in Atlanta. They had been pursuing the Dennis Sharp case with a vengeance, calling around to the various arresting officers and forwarding the results of their conversations to Winslow. That was one area of background checking where an established P.I. firm had it all over me, as even when I had access to a client's long distance lines I frequently didn't come across right. The police officer or county clerk on the other end of the phone would be helpful to a point, but Winslow's people could get them to open up in a way I could not. Not yet, anyway.

It was already late when he dropped me and the box of documents off at my place, but my sleep cycle was so messed up from working nights that I was still awake enough to start sifting through it all.

It turned out I didn't have to go through every last bit of it, as one of the later emails was an executive summary of the information to date. The document was pithy without being incomplete or incomprehensible, and I grew more impressed with Winslow's people in Atlanta as I read it. The box contained backup documents when they had been available, but there was surprisingly little information about Dennis Sharp before he turned twenty-one.

Winslow's people had followed Dennis Sharp's childhood and teenage years by tracking his parents, and they had done that using court records. It was not an ideal upbringing, as the Sharps had run afoul of the law in more than one city and been forced to move on regularly. Two years was the longest span of time they spent in any one place while Dennis was growing up, and that was because they had been graduating to what Winslow's analyst referred to as "the long con."

Spending as much time around P.I.'s as I do, I try to avoid jargon because it makes me sound like a buff. The long con, judging from the context of the report, was a sophisticated, long-term confidence game involving a potentially large payoff. It had to, since the long con took time and money to develop, and the report said that it was viewed in grifter circles as not being worth the investment. Too often the target simply walked away in the middle of things, or the final haul was not big enough to show a profit.

Dennis seemed to have attended school in various parts of the country, turning up winning a spelling contest in this newspaper here and hitting a home run in that journal there. He had not graduated from a high school, instead gaining his equivalence degree roughly eight years prior to his arrival in the Panhandle. The report said he had been sixteen at the time, and it sounded as if he had already known how to lie about his age.

The Sharps had finally gone to real prison only a year before, having participated in a complex fraud job involving U.S. Treasury notes. Ignorant of their world up to that point, I found my head shaking now that the tale had moved on to more familiar ground. Bringing Treasury notes into a con game is a reliable way of getting sent to federal prison for a long time, even if the notes in question never existed, and the Sharps had found that out the hard way. With so many indecipherable investment vehicles out on the market, from crazy derivative cocktails to incomprehensible hedging funds, I had to believe they'd opted for Treasury notes because they wanted to add a hint of reliability somewhere in the mix. They were, after all, running a con game.

Dennis had not been with them at the time, but the court situation had become complicated when some documents indicated Dennis was a minor who was about to lose both his parents. He had been forced to appear before a judge to prove that he was in fact twenty-three at the time, and Winslow's analyst speculated that this confrontation had probably been quite humorous. Although there were no details about what Dennis had been doing at the time of his parents' arrest, the question of his age apparently stemmed from that. The judge was on record as believing Dennis had joined the family business in a different town, but he already had two big fish to fry and so let the young man go.

Reviewing his record following his parents' incarceration, it was hard not to look down on his talents as a grifter. He'd been picked up for vagrancy in Texas, panhandling in Louisiana, traveler's check fraud in Alabama, and traveler's check fraud again in Miami. I was interested in the analyst's description of these events, as I expected to learn that Dennis had actually been involved in high-level crime and that the record reflected some kind of plea bargaining. Apparently my suspicions were unfounded, as the police contacted by Winslow's office had been unconcerned about Dennis, considering him an inept drifter who would eventually end up doing serious time.

Even the police in Alabama and Miami were ambivalent about his whereabouts, even though he had given a fake name in both places and was still wanted in Miami. Once again his bargain-basement crimes failed to excite a system overloaded with felonies and serious misdemeanors, and I began to get a glimmer of what had actually transpired in those places.

Dennis was no orphaned puppy, although he could probably play the part when it suited him. He was twenty-three when his parents went away, and demonstrated more than once that he could talk his way around the servants of the law under the right circumstances. While the report did not say this, I suspected he had been reared in the family business, and that pure dumb luck saved him from being implicated in his parents' bad decision with the Treasury notes.

So what did that leave me? A con man who couldn't get out of his own way, as Winslow suggested? Or was this kid something else entirely, something a bit closer to my own experience than I had first realized? I had felt a silly kinship with him at the outset because he was getting by on nothing and getting hassled the entire way, but perhaps his experience was a bit closer to my own.

Maybe the kid was committing low-rent grifter crime because he was trying to fly below the radar, just as I was. I was keeping my income low so that my creditors could not seize any of it, and Dennis might have restricted himself to nickel-and-dime scams in order to avoid attracting attention. Maybe that judge, the one who had found the question of Dennis's age so funny, had warned him against following in his parents' footsteps. Maybe he'd gone as far as to say he'd be watching. The same way my midnight callers were watching.

So where had that left the kid? With a bag of tricks meant for the Big Leagues that would get him tossed out of the minors as soon as he used even one of them. And so he had been forced to adapt, to learn under fire, to make his mistakes and hope he picked it all up one step ahead of the people trying to stop him.

I sat back, beginning to see how this explanation might work. There was a definite curve to the crimes on his record, from not having any money to passing someone else's traveler's checks to passing a lot of someone else's traveler's checks. He'd even altered his travel habits, dropping the straight line running from Texas through Louisiana and Alabama, by jumping all the way down to Miami. Additionally, he'd changed his previous routine by remaining in a state where he had been arrested and was currently a wanted man.

That also helped to explain his appearance in the Panhandle. It was the high season for tourists and college kids, and even though there were plenty of sophisticated places on the Panhandle, things there were generally a bit slower than in Miami. I liked this part best of all, as he seemed to be adopting a hide-in-plain-sight attitude similar to my own. Staying below the radar, keeping busy learning his new trade, and not doing enough to get anybody excited.

Except the Springers were plenty excited, maybe excited enough to have killed him. And whether the phony bail guys were with the Springers or not, they seemed a little excited, too. I was pondering a few possible explanations for this when the phone rang. It was one in the morning, and I half expected it to be Corelli's idiot nephew with a basic question about the cabstand where he'd been moonlighting for years, but it was Winslow.

"Hey, Frank. I hope I didn't wake you." He sounded tired.

"Nah, I'm just going through that stuff you gave me."

"Well, you can stop." He wasn't tired. I had mistaken a tone of contrition for fatigue. "You got me thinking about that Sharp kid, so I made a few calls when I got back here.

"We're getting paid from a previously undiscovered account held by the Sharps under a different name. The feds don't mind because it's not a huge amount of money and the Sharps are finally cooperating, but that's not the important part.

"Dennis Sharp had access to that account as well. I had some of my people check it out, and he never took out much, but the whole time he's been a street person he's had almost fifty thousand dollars if he needed it."

"Fifty thousand dollars? He was jailed for vagrancy in Texas!"

"Like you said tonight, it doesn't make a lot of sense, does it? But here's the good part. He was making deposits as well. Nothing big, but a thousand here and a few hundred there. And that's from a con man who couldn't walk and chew bubble gum without getting arrested."

"You think he might have been involved in a few things that we don't know about? Things that went his way, and so we'd never hear about them?"

"I'd say that's fairly obvious. We know he got away with something that brought the Springers down on him, too, so who knows? Maybe this street person M.O. was just another con."

"I thought of that. I think he was trying to stay low-key, but it was hard for him because he knew he could do better than that."

"That explains the twenties he handed to Billy Lee like they were printed on disintegrating paper."

"So any news about the two other guys?"

"No, I tried to get in touch with Spears, but it was too late and they refused to call him at home. My guess is there's nothing yet from that angle."

"So what do you want to do?"

"I think we should both get some sleep, and tomorrow go back to that motel and start asking questions all over again."

"Got it. How's nine sound?"

"I'll be by with the coffee. And Frank—" He cleared his throat noisily. "You were right about this kid, and you stuck to your guns, too. That's twice you've kept me from making a big mistake."

"Hey, you're the one who thought of checking on that bank account." Not knowing about the account, I could not speculate if I would have come up with that idea.

"Okay. See you in a few hours. This one just keeps on getting stranger and stranger." He hung up.

I hung up, too, now feeling like I could actually get some shut-eye. I turned, and that was when things really got strange.

Sally Hayes was looking at me through the living-room window.

SHE MADE ME LET HER IN through the back door, which was difficult because most of my few remaining possessions were stacked in front of it in boxes. The house was a nice little place, but it had a minor drawback in that there was very little storage. I tried to convince her to go around front, but as we were conversing with hand signals it didn't get very far.

She burst through the door and into my arms as soon as I had cleared a path. She was dressed in a pair of pink sweatpants meant for someone half her size and the same T-shirt she'd been wearing the night before. Her hair hung loose enough to sweep across my nose even though it was not very long, and for someone reputedly living on the street she smelled pretty good.

"Frank, Frank, you've got to help me!" She clung to me tightly, and while this was not unpleasant I had to remind myself that this was the same girl who could enter a room, sit and eat a sandwich, and leave without touching anything that would take a fingerprint.

"Easy there, easy," I said uncomfortably, feeling her tremble and considering for a moment that she might actually be in trouble. "What's happened?"

I tried to pry her loose, but she was a lot stronger than her size said she'd be, and she locked on fiercely.

"These two guys, they came by and said Dennis owed them some money, and now they say I owe it to them! I don't know what they're talking about, Frank!"

"It's okay, it's okay," I offered, trying to regain control of the situation. Things like this don't usually happen at my place, and never at one in the morning. I finally got a good grip on her upper arms and pushed her back a few inches. She'd definitely been crying, and she looked ready to have a nervous breakdown, so

I put an arm around her before leading her into the living room.

"Close the drapes," she whispered, indicating the side window where she'd gotten my attention a few minutes before. The front window blinds were already drawn, and I complied even though I doubted anyone would see her from my neighbor's yard.

She was staring at the documents spread across my coffee table when I turned around, and it was even money if she would run straight out the front door or not. She looked up with her hands clasped in front of her.

"What are these? Where did you get them?" She stared at me with the eyes of a rabbit caught in a snare.

"It's all right, this is what I do for a living." I started scooping the papers together. "The cabstand is my night job. I'm a fact-checker for local law firms, and sometimes for private investigators, too. I was concerned about what happened to your boyfriend and so I did a little looking around."

The blue eyes widened, and the voice was barely audible, but the sound of hope was unmistakable.

"Are you trying to help me, Frank?"

She stood there wringing her hands, and she was so helpless and teary-eyed and beautiful that I would have said yes even if it were in no way true.

"I don't know what I can do for you, Sally, but yes, I've been helping the police—" I remembered the sketch and quickly found a copy among the items in the folder, and I held it out to her "—and this is a sketch they made of the two men who were asking about your boyfriend at the cabstand."

She let out a startled peep and took a step back as if the paper were going to bite her.

"That's them! That's them! Did you say they were asking about Dennis?"

"Yeah." Having kept her existence a secret from the police, I had forgotten that I had not told her of the visit from the phony bail bondsmen. Between that omission and my embarrassing failure to tell Billy Lee about Dennis Sharp's murder, it might have been time to work harder at getting some shut-eye. "I thought I mentioned that. Sorry. Anyway, the police came by the cabstand when they found out your boyfriend had taken a ride in one of our taxis, and I described the two guys who had been by the night before." I held up the sketch. "These two guys spoke to you? Today?"

She nodded with her gaze fixed on the paper, and I decided to put it away. At least we now knew that the two people Winslow most wanted to meet were still in the area.

"Sally, for goodness' sake, sit down. You're safe here."

She obeyed mechanically, overcome by the events of the past few days, I suppose, and as it was a couch I almost reached out for her again. Winslow's tales of teen runaways with concealed weapons popped into my head at that moment, and so I stayed at my end of the sofa.

"Sally, what did the two men say to you?"

"They said that Dennis was holding some money for them, it was in a small bag when they gave it to him, and that they wanted it back. They said they didn't care that he was—" she couldn't bring herself to say it, and just continued "—and they were sure he had it with him when he rode in that taxi. They think he hid it somewhere, and they want to know where the taxi took him."

So that was why they were still asking about the man they killed. Allegedly killed. They wanted whatever had been in the mysterious bag that they were sure he'd been carrying. They'd asked about it when they met me, pretending to be looking for Dennis, and now they had set the girl on its trail as well.

"Where did you meet these two?"

"At Graner. I didn't have anyplace else to go, the only people I know are there, I thought I'd be safe…"

"They came right up to you at the beach?"

"There's a stone wall with trees behind it, that's where we hang out." I had never been there, but I could imagine the scene. The sand nearly deserted because you don't go to Graner Beach to swim or lay out. An old, cracked seawall covered with graffiti and the legs of dozens of teens, some local and some not, seated on top of it. A constantly changing assortment of young faces, hands passing the odd illegal substance, and every now and then some older faces as well.

"Did they hurt you?"

"No. They didn't even try to cut me out from the rest or anything. That was the scary part. They walked right up, told me they were friends of Dennis, and then told me that if I didn't find out where that bag of money was…you have to help me, Frank!"

She launched herself across the short distance, the tanned arms wrapping around my neck, the taut little torso pressed against mine, and the words, hypnotic, in my ear.

"You know where he went, Frank. You can help me. Help me, Frank."

This might have gone on for some time had the phone not rung. I managed to get myself loose and headed for the phone, resolving to stay standing for the remainder of this visit.

It was Corelli's nephew, somehow unaware of what time it was, calling to let me know that Billy Lee had swung by on his way home. While it escaped me how Billy Lee could have left such a message without telling Corelli's nephew that I was the one who found him, it provided a much needed breathing space.

Hanging up, I remembered Winslow's amusement at Sally Hayes's ability to move through the world without leaving a fingerprint. I considered offering her a glass of water, but somehow couldn't do it. I told myself that she would simply refuse the offer, but the real truth was I couldn't betray the trust she seemed to have in me.

Winslow would say it was all an act, but I would hate myself if it wasn't.

"Sally, where are you supposed to meet these guys? If you get the information they want?"

Her eyes lit up, and she slid forward on the sofa in expectation of some kind of final revelation.

"You can find out where he went, Frank? Or do you already know?"

That last sentence completely broke the spell. The walls suddenly seemed very real around me, and I looked at the curtain on the side window, now shut. Something in those deep blue eyes jumped all on their own, and the animal analogy didn't seem so alluring anymore. Still there, but with a lethal, hungry, predatory feel.

With Billy Lee back in play, and me alone with a total stranger, it seemed like an appropriate time to lie.

"I did check, Sally, but we don't have a record of that trip."

There was a dead silence for a few ticks of the clock, and she stood up suddenly, a single movement with surprising speed. She seemed on the verge of leaving.

"Sally, it's time we went to the police. I know the chief here in Exile, he's a very smart guy—"

"No, thanks, Frank." It was a hard voice, an older woman's voice, and I felt a pang of regret that I had somehow let her down. The voice was gone an instant later, and the childlike expression was back. She smiled at me kindly. "Thanks for everything, Frank, but I gotta go."

She used her T-shirt to open the back door.

I CALLED WINSLOW AS SOON as she was gone. He'd clearly been asleep, but when I described the action he came to in a hurry.

"Frank, I want you to stop letting strangers into the booth or your house. No matter how pretty they are." The words were light, but his tone was not.

"Now, that's not what's going on here. Believe me..."

"I noticed you didn't let the two ugly guys in your office."

"I let you in, didn't I?"

"Touché." He got that out while laughing. "But whoever is playing whom here, we need to get a message to Billy Lee right away to be on his toes. Our friend Dennis obviously had something they wanted, and they seem to have it narrowed down to the time he took that taxi ride."

"I was thinking about that. You don't suppose he actually boosted some of the drugs from that car, and that's what they're after?" Although Sally had said the bail guys were after money, so many people had told me so many stories by then that I was taking the lie for granted.

"With the cops watching? I doubt it."

"You know, we're not sure when they started watching that car, are we?"

"Good point." The words came across as if he had pulled the receiver away from his face while saying them. I figured he was putting something together, and let him think. When he came back on his voice was a tad higher. "As a matter of fact, that's a very good point. So here's a change in plans. I'll pick you up at eight, and we're headed back to the Davis police department.

"We're going to lay out all the cards this time, let them see that something else is going on here, and that they'd better get serious if they don't want to get embarrassed."

"All the cards? The girl, too?"

"Absolutely. We've got a picture of her. She's either working with these guys or being worked by them, and now we've got some bait to bring them out."

I didn't see how the bait could be me, but I also didn't see how it could be anybody else, so I asked.

"Who's the bait?"

"Our good buddy Billy Lee."

WINSLOW'S STATEMENT SOUNDED a bit insensitive, but Billy Lee had already shown he could protect himself, and every cab driver in the area now had a picture of the two gentlemen in question. Ruby had been quite busy distributing the copies, and even though no one had seen anything worth reporting, a large number of cabbies were now on the lookout.

Their vigilance was not due to any conventional civic-mindedness, unless you consider the brotherhood of taxi drivers to be a community, but more on the level of a general dislike for debt collectors and people who were just asking too many questions. More than one guy driving a hack in the Panhandle was avoiding a troubled past in some other part of the country, and so by helping to protect Billy Lee they were indirectly helping themselves.

Getting back to the matter of Billy Lee's safety, Winslow and I were at the Davis police station at nine the next morning trying to sell them on the idea of watching him. And halfway through that discussion I saw that we were putting our own freedom at risk while attempting to make that sale.

"I'd like to know who you contacted in Mobile," Winslow said abruptly, after learning that the police in Mobile had no idea who the guys in the sketch were.

"Since when did we become partners, Winslow?" Spears asked.

"Since you guys tripped the alarm on that drug car."

Winslow let the words hang in the air. He was taking an awful chance, making that statement in front of me and the detectives who had confessed it to him in confidence. It did not take a big imagination to see that he was threatening to pass this knowledge to Baxter's defense attorney.

It also did not take a big imagination to see that we could both be arrested for interfering in a police investigation for even suggesting this, and I hoped Winslow knew what he was doing. He seemed cool enough, sitting there in the dark suit, but it was hard to know if his raised voice was an act or the real thing.

Spears was a different man from the day before. He looked like he hadn't slept well, and his replies that morning had been sullen and disjointed. Several times he had seemed ready to threaten us with the interference charges, but for some reason he was holding himself in check. He probably believed that arresting us would turn the chance of Winslow contacting Baxter's defense team into a certainty, and it was killing him. He looked at me and then back to Winslow.

"Let's take another walk."

"No. Frank has run down more of this case than you and me combined. He's currently working for my firm, and if he tells anybody about this I'll personally give him what we old-timers used to call a Detroit stop-and-frisk." He turned a scowling face toward me, just enough so the other three didn't see him wink. "Besides, I don't feel like walking anywhere."

"Okay, but we are completely off the record here. Understand?" Neither of us answered, so Spears just went ahead. Both Mayfair and Ramirez noticeably sagged in their chairs as the words came out. "When we got the tip from the Springers, it was a description of the car and the license plate number. They told us the car would be coming to a rest stop on the highway at the edge of town between two and three in the morning, and that a drug buy would take place there. We were supposed to keep the place under surveillance and nab the buyer and the seller all at once."

A bombshell. They had not just jumped the gun by setting off Baxter's car alarm at the Seaview; they had completely departed from the script prepared by the Springers. The tip they'd received involved Baxter's car, all right, but at a different place and time. And with a different driver.

Spears went on, his voice getting softer and softer. "But we didn't trust these guys—"

"Gee. Why not?" asked Winslow in a monotone.

"—and so we ran the plate. It was a corporate car, legitimate office-supply business in Tampa, nothing wrong with it. That, of course, made it a good choice for smuggling, and we were concerned that it might come through town early. So we put the information out to our patrol cars."

Winslow couldn't believe his ears. "As what?"

"As exactly what we thought it was: A potentially dangerous situation that had to be kept under surveillance. We warned our guys not to approach it, but to report if they saw it and keep it in sight."

"So that's how you ended up at the Seaview."

"Exactly." I didn't think Spears could lean any farther across the desk, but he did at this point. "You have got to keep this quiet. This case is already hanging by a thread, and nothing we did changes the fact that Baxter is a drug smuggler and that the car was loaded with dope. So what if we jumped the gun? Ever think what would have happened if that story about the rest stop was baloney? What if we had watched that rest stop all night while Baxter drove merrily on by? We had a bird in the hand, and we took it."

"Good police work, if you ask me," Mayfair said supportively.

"Sure, except it kept you from seeing the connection between Dennis Sharp and the Springers. Sharp was supposed to steal that car and take it to that rest area. He was supposed to be sitting there waiting for a Springer connection who would never arrive, and when he gave up and tried to drive off you guys would have arrested him at the wheel of a car loaded with drugs. Just like the Springers wanted."

"You say. I say we intercepted a dangerous drug shipment," Ramirez snapped.

"Except three people still on the loose seem to think Dennis Sharp spirited away something valuable from that car."

"We had to chop that car practically in half to find those drugs."

"Might not have been drugs. Maybe there was a sack of money in that car. Maybe Baxter took it into his room—"

"Uh-uh. We searched his room right after arresting him."

"You're not listening. Three people are trying awfully hard to establish what Dennis Sharp did in the last hours of his life, so regardless of how he did it, or what he stole, we need to assume these three people are not searching for something that isn't there.

"I think the kid got the money, or some of the drugs, or whatever, *before* you arrested Baxter. He was pulling a double cross on the Springers. He stashed the stuff somewhere and came back. He was then going to steal the car and deliver it just like they told him to, but you people interrupted him. So he caught a cab, went to the drop spot where he was supposed to find out where to take the car, and decided to cut his losses and run off with the cash instead."

"So who killed him?"

"My money's still on the two guys in the sketch, but it may even have been sweet little Sally Hayes. All three of them are trying to find out where Dennis went after the police showed up, and all three of them have asked if he was carrying anything when he flagged down the cab. As of one this morning they're still looking for the cab driver, and now the cab driver's back out on the road.

"So what say you put a tail on Billy Lee, flood the area with the pictures of all three of our suspects, and wrap this thing up?"

EIGHT

WE DIDN'T HANG AROUND TO oversee the arrangement of Billy Lee's new shadows. Spears had agreed to begin watching him immediately, and to put out the word for the local police to be on the lookout for the two bail bonds guys and Sally Hayes.

"You didn't really mean that in there, did you? About the girl killing her boyfriend?" I asked as we went down the road toward the Seaview.

"Frank, I was a cop too long to rule anything out. You wouldn't believe some of the things I've seen, and it's just gotten worse since I became a P.I. Husbands killing wives, wives killing husbands, and those were what you'd call normal, stable relationships. These two kids, one's a con man and the other's a runaway. I would not be surprised in the least if she did it.

"After all, if anybody was going to know about Dennis Sharp's hush-hush job that night, it would be her, right?"

"She hasn't mentioned it either time I've spoken with her. According to her, he said he'd meet her at this beach, Graner Beach, later that night. It was almost as if he were putting her safely out of the way."

"Maybe. We still haven't established the nature of

her relationship to the two bail bonds guys." He lightly punched the steering column in a gesture of frustration. "And if our helpers in the Davis P.D. had just gotten that sketch out like we asked, we might actually have those two in custody by now instead of starting at square one."

"You think this surveillance on Billy Lee is going to turn them up?"

"Maybe, maybe not. It's just that if we had them in custody they'd be facing accessory-to-a-murder rap, so if they didn't do it you can bet they'd clear up the relationship to the girl. But regardless of that, don't forget whoever killed him was waiting for him when he went back to get his things. Sweet little Sally would know where that was."

An important observation came into focus for me at that instant, and I twisted in my seat.

"Curt, I just thought of something. Both the bail guys and Sally have been asking if Dennis was carrying something when he left the motel. The bail guys are telling Sally that Dennis had some of their money and they want it back. And both groups are trying to figure out where Dennis went that night after leaving the Seaview."

"Right."

"So if they were waiting for him at his hiding place and killed him there, why didn't they just ask him then?"

THINGS GOT BUSY RIGHT AFTER that. Despite my advice against it, Winslow departed almost immediately for

Mobile to go see the Springers. He was fed up with relying on the Davis P.D. and had apparently laid the groundwork for such a meeting through another member of his firm with the right contacts. He was polite when he turned down my offer to go along.

"Frank, no offense, but if there's a sit-down it's only going to be one guy from our side. The Springers have been implicated in a drug snatch that ended up with a dead body, and you can bet they're not going to discuss that with more than one person, if at all."

"Then why go? Your contact doesn't even know who they'll send." Although Winslow was confident that he was in no danger, I could see a number of ways that this could go wrong. Maybe you have to be an ex-cop from Detroit to view a meeting with gangsters in Mobile, Alabama, as a safe venture, but speaking as an ex-computer programmer from Connecticut I was concerned.

He did give me something to do, though, before heading out. The Davis P.D. had let him down so badly that he wasn't taking any chances on their ability to locate the girl. Sally had mentioned Graner Beach twice in the space of two meetings with me, and Winslow felt there was some chance that I might be able to spot her if I stayed far enough away.

"And I mean stay away, Frank. I know you think this girl is innocent, and maybe she is, but for all we know she's working hand in hand with those other two guys. If you see her, call the police. They said they were looking for her, so hold them to it.

"And keep your eyes peeled for those other two jokers. I don't want them sneaking up on you while you're checking out the scene at the beach. Remember, as far as they're concerned you can help them get what they want, and I bet they won't be shy about asking for it."

"I'll be careful if you will," I said meaningfully, and we clasped hands. We'd already gone over the phone numbers once more and promised to be in touch, but I watched him go with a fair amount of dread that I would not be seeing him again.

And as much as I wanted to head to Graner Beach and check out the scenery, I knew there was one place where I needed to check in before that. I whistled up a Midnight cab and headed back to Exile.

GRAY TOLIVER WAS A RETIRED Navy petty officer who had spent the back half of his career in Pensacola and chosen Exile as the place to spend his golden years. I had met him at the Exile public beach, where he played chess most mornings. He was there when I rolled up, even though he was none too happy to see me.

As the first real friend I had made in my first few months in the Panhandle, Gray had proven an invaluable source of advice in the earlier Gonzalez case. A man of wide experience and inexhaustible knowledge, he had helped to design and test the wings of many Navy planes, and he could simplify extraordinarily complex issues like no one else I had ever encountered.

He was packing up his set of heavy pewter chessmen on a table at the beachside park when I walked up. Along with picnic tables and trash barrels, the park was outfitted with these nifty concrete table-and-chair arrangements on which a checkerboard was etched, which alleviated the need to bring a board. Gray and I had spent many hours there when I had first hit town, and he was the first stranger whom I had told of my misfortunes up north.

Although well into his retirement, Gray had no physical difficulties and kept his body as toned as his mind. He was wearing a weathered blue shirt untucked over white shorts, and with his white hair and deep tan he looked like Hemingway's Old Man of the Sea. He looked at me the same way the old fisherman had looked at the sharks as they devoured the biggest catch of his life.

"Well, well, if it isn't the cabstand guy. Where's your hat, cabbie?" The tone was not friendly. I had not been by for some time, and even though Gray knew I had taken a second job he was always hungry for tales from my real occupation.

"Back at the stand. How about a game?"

"Sorry, cabbie. Business hours just ended. Maybe if you came by a little more frequently you'd know that."

"Okay, forget the game. Gray, I need your help."

"Help? You in trouble, or you just humoring an old man?"

"Neither. But I've got a case that's scattered all to heck and gone, it doesn't make any sense to me, and you've always been able to sort out things like that. So whaddya say? Care to give it a try?"

"This from your fact-checking work, or some silly cabstand thing?"

"Both, actually. A kid who hailed one of our cabs ended up dead over in Davis, and you wouldn't believe how many people have come by asking about him."

That did it. The Old Man of the Sea had the hook in his mouth. Gray's angry face shifted into the look of an art expert caught in the middle of an appraisal.

"Dead? A local?" Gray was a transplant just like me, but you didn't live in Denny Dannon's town for long without learning to look out for your neighbors.

"No. A runaway. Son of two incarcerated con artists, and maybe working for a gang of real rough types from Mobile."

"The Springer gang?" He was sitting down by then, and motioned me to do the same. Gray read every local newspaper cover to cover every day, and probably knew more about the Springers than the Davis P.D.

"That's them. There's a P.I. from Atlanta talking with them even as we speak, and in a second you'll see why…"

"THAT WAS GREAT. THANK you, Frank." Gray sounded as if he'd just eaten a gourmet meal instead of hearing my convoluted description of the case to date. "And congratulations. In town only a year and you've already got two girlfriends. Even if one is probably underage and might kill you at any moment.

"Come to think of it, Beth Ann might kill you, too, if she happens across you and Blondie in a clutch."

"Gimme a break, Gray."

"Okay, okay." Gray had a good sense for when I wasn't in a mood for his usual lecturing. I don't think he recognized that I was working on my second day without sleep.

"Here's what you do." Gray reached into the roomy canvas shoulder bag that he used to transport the chess pieces. He came up with a legal pad and a pen, and quickly began drawing a series of parallel lines, both vertical and horizontal, separating the top sheet into some sort of matrix. He began writing little notes across the top and down the left side of the paper, labeling the rows and columns. He tore that sheet off, passed it to me, and kept writing on the next page.

I looked down and saw an empty grid with labels across the top and down one side. The names of the players went across the top, notations such as "The Kid," "The Bail Guys," and "Davis P.D." Down the left-hand side things got a little more complicated, as I was supposed to complete the grid for designations such as "Location before drug bust," "Location during drug bust," and one that was simply called "Name." For instance, I would have a lot of empty boxes under the "The Bail Guys" column because I did not know where the "bail guys" had been at any time except our one meeting, but I would be able to say that Dennis Sharp was at the Seaview before the drug bust.

"What's this one here? The one called 'Name'?"

"That one's important. Think hard when you fill that out." Gray was still writing up another grid, this one a basic timeline showing the players down the left-hand side and the events of the night of the robbery across the top.

"With what? What name?"

"Why, Dennis Sharp's name, of course. For each of those people, he was Dennis Sharp or Dennis Taylor. When this P.I. came to see you, he thought the kid's name was Taylor. When the bail guys came by, they told you his name was Sharp." He took the paper back and wrote "Taylor" in the "Name" row of the "Winslow" column, and "Sharp" in the "The Bail Guys" line.

"In fact, if the bail guys hadn't told you his name was Sharp, you'd never have found out that his folks are in jail. You had nothing else to use, no information, no fingerprints, no police bulletin. You found all of this because those two knuckleheads told you his name was Sharp. Key."

"We might not have figured that out for a long time, either, because he hadn't used the name Sharp since leaving Louisiana. Even though the police in Miami and 'bama had identified him by his prints, we wouldn't have come across that information without knowing his name was Sharp."

"Keep filling that out." He began working on the second matrix using what I had told him, but stopped when he saw I wasn't writing anymore. I had only completed the "Name" row, but it told a tale all its own.

Gray had arranged the grid so that each piece of information for a given player would be side by side with the same category for every other player. In this case, the "Name" row went straight across the page with the word "Taylor" in every box except two. Forced to remember by this simple paper drill, I could now see that the only people who identified Dennis by his real name were his girlfriend and the two bail guys. The box for the Springers was empty, as I had no idea what name they knew him under.

"There you go," Gray murmured, pointing at the paper. "So now you need only one thing: What name did the Springer gang have for him? If they knew him as Sharp, there's a chance your two bail guys are working for them. In that case they knew his name was Sharp because the Springer gang told them.

"But if the Springer gang knew him as Taylor, or Turner, or anything but Sharp, your two bail guys are working with the kid's girlfriend. She'd know his real name for obvious reasons, and if they didn't get that from Mobile, they got it from her."

He looked up from the pages and got my attention.

"Remember that next time she tries to give you a hug."

GRAY MADE ME PROMISE TO finish the remaining five pages of grids before letting me go.

"Just because you found one important item in the

first grid you worked on doesn't mean there aren't more. You need a way of sorting your findings so they aren't this jumbled mass of conflicting information. That's the only way you're going to figure this out."

I didn't tell him that a twelve-hour shift in the booth at the cabstand was going to leave me plenty of time to do my homework. I thanked him and left after giving my word that I would keep him informed of my progress.

I tried to call Winslow twice, once with Gray sitting there and once in the car, but his cell phone was beyond the calling area. I needed to tell him to find out the name by which the Springers knew Dennis Sharp, but thus far I hadn't even been able to leave him a message.

My next move was a toss-up between having a look at Graner Beach or going to have a second look at the Seaview. I was going to need a set of binoculars if I chose Graner, so I swung by my place to pick them up.

As it turned out, there was no need to leave a message for Winslow after all.

I didn't recognize the man when I saw him sitting on my porch. The stranger was tall and quite old, with red blotches on cheeks that looked like they were made from paper and cobwebs. He was dressed in a short-sleeved peach guayabera, light gray cotton trousers that were too big for him, dress shoes, and a brimmed straw hat. A dark brown cane was propped between his knees, with a handle that looked so much like the grip on a pistol that at first I believed he was holding a spear gun.

I approached slowly, and saw alert blue eyes tracking me before the man smiled. His teeth were intact, but set in that ruin of a body they seemed out of place. I guessed that if you put us both together we wouldn't add up to three hundred pounds.

"Hello, Mr. Cole. I hope you don't mind that I decided to wait for you out of the sun." No matter how he looked, the voice was deep, Southern, and educated. He spoke in a slow, decided fashion, as if the pronunciation of the individual words was important to him.

"I'm afraid you have me at a disadvantage."

"Always a good thing." He stuck out his hand without getting up. "Pardon me for not rising, but as you can see I left middle age behind a few ages ago. My name is Elijah Springer, and I would like to talk to you."

Several questions occurred to me at that moment, all involving whether or not this man knew that Curtis Winslow was supposed to be meeting representatives of his group in Mobile. I did not think this aged gentleman had come to my place by accident, and so it made sense to simply go ahead and ask.

"Nice to meet you, Mr. Springer. I've heard a few things about a Springer family in Mobile recently—"

"My relations. And yes, Frank, I know your friend Detective Winslow is scheduled to meet with some of our people this afternoon in Mobile. Sadly, that meeting will not take place, but that is why I am here.

"I hope this does not come as a shock, but I did not consider it wise for my nephews to meet with Detective Winslow concerning the matter of young Dennis Taylor, rest in peace. I felt it would be a safer thing for everyone if I met with you here."

"Me?"

"Please don't be offended, Mr. Cole, but as a novice investigator your worth on a witness stand is questionable at best. Whereas the testimony of a retired police officer, a much decorated police officer, by the way, currently working as a private investigator for a top-notch firm might be considered quite credible."

I leaned back against the solid wooden wall which ran around my front porch. Far from being insulted, I felt like a little kid who has been invited to go do something with a revered older brother and his friends. Judging from Springer's last statement, he meant to convey some important information to me and was concerned that it might be repeated in a court of law.

"Not that anything I tell you is admissible, anyway. In fact, you could record our conversation and it would do you no good. You see, I was declared legally insane a number of years ago, a condition which qualified me for the role of go-between in circumstances such as these."

"You seem quite lucid to me."

"Oh, I have my moments, as the court decision itself admits, but not of such duration and frequency to make a difference. But we digress.

"Mr. Cole, I have traveled here to tell you that my relations had nothing to do with the death of Mr. Taylor."

Even if everything he'd said up until then was pure hokum, at least there was a fair indication that the other Springers knew Dennis Sharp as Dennis Taylor.

"I don't mean to insult you, sir, but why would I accept your denial? According to the Davis police, someone who may be related to you tipped them off about that drug shipment."

"No insult taken, young man. Though I am not very current as far as family matters are concerned, if someone did assist the police in thwarting such a crime, it would be in the way of fulfilling a civic duty. Not to mention, the people who sent that car here are a loathsome collection of vicious thugs from outside this country, and it serves everyone's interests that they be discouraged from moving north."

"North as in the Panhandle."

"Exactly. In Mobile we prefer to think that this part of the country will continue as a nice, quiet place."

"So why did you tell the kid to steal the drug car when you'd already tipped off the police?"

"I should think that was obvious."

"It is. You wanted him behind bars."

"Indeed. You see, Mr. Cole, in the old days we had a limited number of responses to people like Mr. Taylor. Sadly, none of those responses worked very well as far as passing the word that grifters should avoid us.

"It's one of the unsettling quirks of the grifter mind

that they don't respect an outright execution. It is simply not effective to kill one of them, but it is highly instructive to trick one of them. In other words, a dead confidence man is simply a corpse, while a grifter tricked into prison is an object lesson."

"And that's supposed to convince me? You didn't kill him because it wasn't good enough?"

"Pass it along to Mr. Winslow. He might understand."

"The kid was killed after the deal went wrong. Your explanation doesn't fit."

"Be careful, young man. I was not always a messenger. And attached to the handle of this cane is an eighteen-inch piece of stainless steel shaped like an ice pick. I may be old, but if I got sufficiently annoyed, I could drive that steel straight through a telephone pole."

I considered that statement for a good five seconds before deciding to answer. I kept it deadpan, as I really didn't want to see what was inside his cane.

"Do the telephone poles ever get you that mad?"

He roared with laughter.

"That was very funny, Frank! Very funny indeed!" He laughed so hard that he was finally forced to produce a brightly colored silk handkerchief and cough into it violently. He came back up none the worse for wear, and continued without missing a beat. "I can see you have perspective, young man. People with senses of humor always have perspective. That's what's missing in our district attorneys these days. Way back when, the D.A.'s had perspective. They could appreciate a joke."

Not knowing what joke used a foot-and-a-half-long ice pick for a prop, I asked a question that had been bothering me since his sudden appearance.

"Mr. Springer, one last thing: Why are you talking to us at all?"

"Mr. Cole, right now Mr. Baxter is looking at a long time in prison and might even be convinced to name some names in Miami. However, if the connection between the boy, the car, and the idiotic Davis police department is brought up in court, Baxter may walk away a free man.

"We didn't kill the boy, and so the best outcome for us is for you to find out who did. That way Mr. Winslow will go back to Atlanta, Mr. Baxter will go to jail, and no one will need know about this unfortunate coincidence."

He took out a flip phone and hit a speed dial button. He then closed the lid without speaking into the device, and a moment later a large dark car with smoked windows came down the road in our direction. He rose and shook my hand.

"Good luck, Mr. Cole." He looked around him. "In your dealings with the police, it might help to know that usually a large amount of cash was in Mr. Baxter's car along with the contraband. We couldn't help noticing it wasn't mentioned in the papers."

It was too late in the day for a trip to Graner, so I went in early to the cabstand even though I was not going to spell Corelli a minute before my scheduled time. I asked him to wake me when that time came and, barely able to keep my eyes open, I curled up on the backseat of a taxi that was kept on the lot as a kind of movable rest house. It was an older model with a bench seat, and I fell asleep to the sound of birds in a tree overhead.

It seemed only a moment later that Corelli was shaking me awake, but it was getting dark and so I knew I had slept for at least three hours. Two of those hours had actually been on my shift, but Corelli did not want a zombie for a dispatcher. His wife had finally called, and so he woke me, presented me with a large cup of coffee, and walked me over to the booth before leaving.

It took me a long time to wake up. My mouth felt dry even with the coffee, and things around me seemed in slow motion. Ruby called in a fare, and I had to make him repeat it twice before getting it down correctly. Only the realization that I had failed to contact Winslow with my news finally managed to wake me, and I dialed his number.

"Winslow." He answered in a low voice, and I heard the sound of traffic behind the voice.

"Curt, it's Frank. I have news."

"Can it wait? I'm about to meet someone."

"From that family? You sure about that?"

"Yes, Frank, I think I'd know who I'm meeting. Been at this all day, too, so what's the news?"

"One of their people came to see me. An old guy—" His voice had suggested that there was someone nearby who could overhear us, so I didn't know if I should use any proper names.

"This old guy have a name, Frank?"

"Yes, Elijah Springer, he—"

"Hang on." I heard him talking in an even lower voice to someone, and he came back on. His voice was louder this time. "Elijah Springer? He's the last one of the founding fathers left alive! He came to see you?"

"Yes, and he said they weren't willing to talk to you, you being an ex-cop and all." I figured it was quicker to say it that way than to explain that he'd make a better witness than I would. "He told me they didn't kill the kid."

"Imagine that."

"So who're you going to meet?"

"One of my firm's people has been doing some arm twisting down here. Got me in with the two honchos, Jack and Al. They're going to pick us up any minute now."

"Us?"

"Yes, the other guy from my firm is here with me. Look, there's a car coming, you at the cabstand?"

"Yeah."

"I'll call you as soon as I'm done here."

"Make sure you do."

"Yes, Mom."

I CALLED BILLY LEE NEXT, using the radio this time. He seemed happy to be driving fares around the Panhandle instead of riding the waves on that charter boat.

"Nothin' to report, Frank. Nobody unusual's taken a ride or asked me any strange questions." I'd warned him of the possibility that the phony bail bondsmen might get someone else to sit in for them, and to be wary of anyone who got nosy. "Matter of fact, I gotta wonder if those Davis police types are out here, either."

"What do you mean?"

"I haven't so much as seen a patrol car near me all night. If they are watching me, they are some kind of supercops. Either that or they're invisible."

He didn't sound terribly concerned, and I suppose that came with the territory. He'd been driving a hack for a few years now, and even though the Panhandle was not a high-crime area, it had its moments. Still, I was a bit surprised that the lack of police protection was not more of a concern for someone in his shoes. But that was Billy Lee all over: Tell him a bill collector is asking for him and he flees the state, but tell him a guy with a gun might hop in his cab and he shrugs it off.

"Billy Lee, would you mind checking in with me through the night? For me?" I tried to sound like Chief Dannon and failed.

"Now, what are the fares gonna think, Frank? That they drew the newest driver in the Midnight Taxi Service, a guy so green he has to keep reporting to base to tell them he hasn't done anything wrong yet?"

"Speaking as the newest guy in the Midnight Taxi Service, I don't see anything wrong with that."

"You? You don't qualify as the newest guy until you get a hack license."

"Hey, Frank?" Tony Ng's voice came over the radio.

"Yeah, Tony." We were a little weak on proper radio procedure at the Midnight stand.

"I just wanted to call and let you know I'm okay. I'm at Fourth and Main…no, now it's Fifth and Main…wait a minute, hang on, okay, now it's Sixth—"

"Okay, let's cut the chatter. Open Mike Night's not 'til Tuesday," Ruby's voice broke in. He must have had a van full of people to do that, as he normally let the comedians in the group rant away at will.

"Sorry, Rube." It was Danny, in the blue van.

"Danny, you weren't even talking just now."

"I know."

"Then what are you apologizing for?"

The radio went quiet then, and even though it was a busy night I got through a lot of the homework Gray had assigned me. The grids slowly began to fill with inked-in notes about who was where at what time and what they were doing, and it began to organize my thinking. Normally I was not keen on matrices, having worked with too many project managers who churned them out by the ton, but this time it helped.

For example, one whole grid was dedicated to how different people had traced Dennis to the Midnight Service. Filling it out was easy, but so many of the people listed on the left-hand side of that matrix had been lying that the overall value of the grid was in question. I focused on the people who were probably not lying to us, and then began studying how the Davis P.D. had connected the kid to us.

According to Spears, one of the street maps carried by our drivers had been in the kid's pocket when his body was discovered. The street map had the Midnight logo on it, and so the police had shown up at the stand. Billy Lee had confirmed this story, having given the map to Dennis Sharp when the kid got whatever message had been left for him at the weigh station.

This got me thinking about the message he'd received that night. The phone at the weigh station didn't work, and Sharp was carrying a cell phone anyway, so it sounded like some kind of message drop like you see in spy movies. Presumably the message had told him to go somewhere unfamiliar, and so Sharp had asked for a street map. He'd tucked the map in his pocket, but what had happened to the message?

Had he thrown it away? That might make sense, as he had failed to steal the car as instructed, and in any event did not go where he had been directed. He had disappeared into a crowd at the boardwalk and gone to get his things at his campground instead, probably in preparation for flight, and so it was possible that he had simply thrown the message away.

But maybe not. Concern about his survival that night had prompted Dennis to leave his parents a taped message telling them where he had been, and what he had been doing. The purpose of that tape was to give them a start point when they sent someone looking for him, and the Seaview Motel was that start point. Curt Winslow had tracked him to the Midnight Service because a suspicious desk clerk had seen him flag down Billy Lee's cab, but that now seemed an unlikely thing for a man in mortal danger to count on.

If the clerk hadn't seen him, the clue about the motel would have been a dead end. That didn't sound like the trail left by a practitioner of the long con, and I began to get an itch to see inside the motel room the kid had rented. A clue left in that room would make more sense, and would also go a long way toward explaining why he had rented the place. I scratched that down on a separate list of things to do, and went back to the question of the message at the weigh station.

When Dennis made the tape for his parents, he hadn't known where he was going from the Seaview. He probably got the instructions to go to the weigh station via cell phone at the last second, maybe even as a Davis plainclothes officer was intentionally bumping into an office-supply salesman's car across the parking lot. Though a little rushed by the appearance of so many police, Dennis still needed to leave a clue behind for whomever his parents sent to the Seaview looking for him. And if the kid had left some kind of clue in his otherwise unnecessary motel room, it probably mentioned the weigh station.

Running out the door, he'd flagged down Billy Lee and gone to get his next set of orders. By then the kid was moving too fast to call up and make another tape for his folks, so he might just have returned the weigh station message to the crack where he found it. If he later found time to make a new tape all this would be unnecessary, but he had no idea how much time he had. Assuming he would not get to make a new tape, he might have returned the weigh station message to its spot for the benefit of anyone following the clue left in the motel room.

The more I considered it, the more it sounded like wishful thinking. The kid had left a message for his folks in case he ended up dead, and they had hired a big P.I. firm to find him. That firm would have kept looking no matter what they learned at the Seaview. In the meantime, the kid was probably on the run right from the moment the police cars entered the parking lot, so it didn't make sense for him to leave clues for the wrong people to find.

The wrong people. The wrong people had left that message for him at the weigh station, and if they were trying to find him after that night, they might check to see if he had even gone there. A man trying to leave no trace of his activities that night would have taken pains to put that note back exactly the way he found it.

I got up and paced around the tiny office. Even if the note was still there, what good would it do? He hadn't gone where he was being told to go. Unless it was signed by Elijah Springer, it wasn't going to do me any good.

There was no reason to pursue it, and that is why I got Billy Lee to drive me to the weigh station as soon as we were done swabbing out the cabs the next morning.

NINE

THE WEIGH STATION WAS A remote, deserted place even in the light of early morning, and I can only imagine how forbidding it must have looked in darkness. Particularly for a con man who was supposed to be at the wheel of a stolen car that he did not have.

The station wasn't even visible from the highway, which did little to increase its attractiveness. That stretch of highway was flanked on both sides with tall pines, and the only indication that a sizable area of pavement ran parallel to the road was a rusting metal sign, pointing to the turnoff that led to a weigh station. Like most weigh stations I have seen, this one was closed.

"Abandoned" was a better term, as the pavement was cracked and whitened, with grass growing through the cracks. The concrete slab on which trucks presumably had been weighed was covered with broken bottles, and a pair of heavy metal I-beams sticking up from the ground was all that was left of the equipment. Standing on the slab and looking toward the highway, I could barely see through the woods. This must have been an awfully lonely place come sundown.

The trees stretched back behind me an unknown distance, although the foliage grew thicker and brighter a few hundred yards out in a way which suggested the presence of a stream. Further up, near the exit back onto the highway, stood a lone telephone pole turned a tan color by the elements. Deep horizontal cracks ran straight into the wood, and a host of ruler-sized splinters waited to catch an unwary hand. A long coiled cable ran from the pole and into the pavement, holding it upright and signaling that this was the end of that particular phone line.

"I was parked farther up, looking out onto the highway. I wasn't any too happy about being out here and wanted to make darn sure I could get back on the road in a hurry if I had to," Billy Lee explained, standing next to the pole to which the phone was affixed.

What amazed me about the phone was not its age, or its rusted condition, or even the empty bird's nest perched atop the tiny Plexiglas roof. What surprised me was that the receiver was still attached, though so scratched and gnarled that it seemed someone had used it to shoe horses.

For fun I lifted the receiver and found that the line was indeed dead as promised. I began looking around the rectangular box of the phone itself, trying to see a spot where a piece of paper could have been jammed. There was nothing there, and a quick look in the coin slot yielded the same result.

"Did he go anywhere else out here, Billy Lee?"

"Nope. I was watchin' him pretty good, concerned as I was that he might be meeting some unsavory people out here, and he didn't go anywhere but this pole." He pointed over our heads to where a dull gray arm supported a teardrop-shaped streetlight. "Believe it or not, that light still works."

I walked around the pole and saw a rusted metal box attached to the wood on the opposite side. It looked like an old police call box I'd seen once as a kid, and I wondered what one of those would be doing out here. I pushed the lid back. The hinge surrendered with a squeal, and a folded piece of notepaper fell out on the ground.

The phone booth had merely been the marker. The actual drop was the call box on the other side, and the kid had been able to access it without attracting Billy Lee's attention. I reached down and picked up the note, seeing it was written on a lined piece of paper torn from a spiral notebook.

"'Go to the Hi-Speed Mall. Park under the trees on the empty side of the parking lot. You'll be met there. Come alone for your friend's sake.'"

I read it twice before speaking.

"Billy Lee."

"Yeah."

"Our little car theft just turned into a kidnapping."

"Kidnapping? Kidnapped who?"

"Exactly."

"IT DOESN'T TAKE A GENIUS to know it was the girl, Frank." At the other end of the phone line Winslow sounded as if he'd been up all night. "Who else would he care about? So the question isn't who was being held hostage, the question is who wrote the note."

"Maybe you can ask the Springers when you see them," I said acidly, still annoyed from his dismissive attitude about Elijah Springer's visit. Winslow had been given the runaround all night, getting driven from here to there for connections and meetings which somehow didn't work out.

"I doubt it was the Springers, Frank," he replied testily. "He was already working for them, so why would they need the insurance?"

"Maybe they were concerned he was going to double-cross them, kind of like they were going to do to him when he showed up with the car."

"Except they told the cops to stake out a completely different place than the one in the note. No, this is somebody else horning in on the action."

"The girl?"

"Why not? She probably knew what he was being asked to do, knew what was in the car, and arranged a phony kidnapping. Probably blamed it on the Springers, too. She probably had somebody like our two bail bonds guys call him up with new instructions. Remember, in two visits she didn't tell you anything about a kidnapping."

"But why would she do something like that?"

"Tired of Dennis, shopping around for a better sugar daddy, who knows?"

"You seem awful sure she's working with those two."

"Me? You're the one who brought up the name thing. And you're absolutely right. She and the two bail guys were the only ones who called him Sharp, and I can't imagine any other way they'd get his name unless it was from her."

"We keep forgetting that he might have told them himself."

"After not using his real name for so long, and knowing that his real name would pop up with a WANTED sign next to it if anybody ran it through a computer? No way.

"Which brings us to my next order of business. So this little side trip to Mobile won't be a total loss, I've got an appointment with the arresting officer for Dennis's check fraud bust. That was the first time that he used an alias to get out of jail, and I'd like to make sure he wasn't using the name Sharp."

"What? You don't think the Springers are gonna call you again?"

He said something unpleasant and signed off.

IT WAS TIME TO START accepting the notion that Sally Hayes had been playing her boyfriend Dennis, in which case I had to figure she'd been playing me, too. The issue of Dennis Sharp's true identity was particularly damaging, as no one seemed to know his real name except the girl and her alleged accomplices. The more I looked at it, the more reasonable it seemed. I mentally reviewed her two visits and couldn't find anything to suggest the suspected connection was in error, and even found something that seemed to confirm it.

Her trip to Exile was what put the final nail in the coffin lid. My house is two towns over from Davis, and even though she probably could have hitched a ride out there, where had she gone when she ran off into the night? I was prepared to believe that a runaway could cover a lot of distance when necessary, but Exile is pretty far out of the way. Getting a taxi at that time of night is difficult, even if you have the money for it, and thumbing for a ride would probably get you an interview with Chief Dannon.

So she'd gotten a lift to Exile from Ames and Knight, and had hopped right back in that car after leaving my place. The notion that I had been alone with her in my house with all the blinds drawn now gave me a certain chill, and that chill got a lot colder when I considered the likely proximity of the two phony bail bondsmen that evening. Anybody who would stage a fake kidnapping to double-cross a hardened con artist would make short work of a skinny fact-checker, and I had to wonder why she hadn't whistled up the available muscle for a more in-depth interview.

I didn't wonder long, as a mental review of the final part of that visit pointed to what had saved me a rough time. I'd convinced her that I had no idea where Billy Lee had taken Dennis that night, and that there was no record of the trip. Sally and her friends had no idea who had driven the cab that night, and so the Midnight

Taxi Service had become a dead end for them. I liked this answer, as it suggested that they might just have decided to head for greener pastures, and when I considered the added difficulty of having their pictures all over town it even made sense.

That was what I was thinking when I rolled into the parking lot of the Seaview Motel for the second time. I almost turned around and headed back toward Exile and a sensible decision to go to bed, but there were still some unanswered questions from the motel and I was already there anyway.

I decided to walk around the place before going into the office with my questions. I should have done this the very first time I was there, simply as a fundamental of good investigating, but I hadn't really been on the case then. Now I was being paid by Winslow's firm, the girl and her friends had brought me into a tangle of lies, and I also had the opportunity to find something without Winslow's aid. That might sound childish, but I wasn't the one who scoffed at the elder Springer's visit to Exile.

The cleaning lady was going about her morning rounds by then. She was working on the ground-floor units, and I came up on her and the cart just as she was closing the door to one of the rooms.

She was an older Caucasian woman, short and solidly built, wearing a midcalf-length service tunic of some navy blue material. Her hair was pulled back in a bun, and what I could see of it used to be dark before it went gray. She looked up at me the same way she would look down at a stopped-up commode, and waited for me to speak.

"Good morning, ma'am, I'm Frank Cole. I'm investigating the drug bust that took place here a few nights ago—"

"Are you a police officer?" The words came out slow and heavily Southern, but that was more in disbelief than anything else. I didn't try to put one over on her for the simple reason that I didn't think it would work.

"Oh, no, ma'am, I do a little background checking for a private investigations firm…"

"If you're not a police officer I'm not going to talk to you. The office is across the lot." She turned to the other side of the cart and made as if to run me over with it.

"I'd surely do that, ma'am, except the folks in the office don't seem to know much."

That brought a hint of a smile on her lips, so I went on.

"For instance, I bet they didn't clean out that man Baxter's unit the next morning. I bet you did, and I would also bet that the police tore that room to pieces."

She turned with a skeptical look on her face, but clearly I was entertaining her. After regarding me long enough to see I would not evaporate, she fished a pack of ladies' cigarettes from the skirt pocket of her tunic and lit up. I waited politely until she exhaled.

"I had to reassemble that bed all by myself. The

frame, I mean. Those silly cops practically destroyed that room. But when I asked old Canfield to help me out, all of a sudden he's got a bad back." I recognized the name of the Seaview's manager.

"Bad back, my eye," she went on. "I once saw him hoist that floozy of his over one shoulder and carry her all the way to his car." She took another long drag. "He's usually a little more careful than that, being married like he is, but I guess the wife was outta town."

She stared at me through another drag and exhalation.

"That the kind of thing you're trying to dig up?"

"Not exactly. Who is the young lady he tossed so easily?" We shared a secret smile as I took out a notebook and pen. I honestly couldn't care less if Canfield was sneaking around, or with whom for that matter, but the maid obviously wanted to get this information into my hands.

"Rita Shafter, a little taller than I am, red hair, a little heavier than I am, if you know what I mean."

It occurred to me that we were conversing in full view of the office window across the lot.

"Um, ma'am, are you comfortable talking to me out in the open like this?"

"Stop calling me ma'am, junior. You Yankees always sound stupid when you try to speak Southern. My name's Joyce Winters, and I am not the least bit afraid of that beanpole. Go ahead and write that down."

"Yes, ma'am, I mean Joyce."

"What else you need?"

"Joyce, you weren't here the night of the arrest, were you?"

"You think I spend my every waking hour here? I've got a whole other job along with this one. No, I wasn't here."

"Did you get to speak with any police when you came in?"

"Sure did. They were all excited about a bag of money that was supposed to be in that car, but turned out not to be there."

"Excuse me?"

"They said there was supposed to be some money hidden in the car, and they were going over the grounds here with a fine-tooth comb looking for it. Seemed to think it was hidden around here somewhere, but they still didn't have it when they left around noon."

She looked down the row at the end unit, the one closest to the street, which Baxter had occupied.

"You been out back? They cut down a big section of the chain link back there so they could go through the old newspapers and bottles and other things that were piled up between the fence and the building. Nothing there, either, looks like, but they sure seemed serious."

It was starting to sound as if Dennis Sharp might just have managed to boost some of Baxter's possessions after all. If the police had searched the room, impounded the car, and then scoured the grounds, it seemed likely that the fabled bag of money had disappeared before they ever got there.

"That about it, sport? I have a little work to do."

I WALKED DOWN THE ROW and took a left turn at the sidewalk. I passed the outside wall of Baxter's last voluntary place of residence, noting the painted words advertising the Seaview's cable television, air-conditioning, and reasonable rates.

The Seaview's next-door neighbor was a one-story appliance shop with big display windows. A chain-link fence ran around three sides of the store's property, ten feet tall and relatively new. On the Seaview's side the barrier ran almost flush with the back wall of the units, which comprised the motel's right arm. Each of these units had a back window facing the fence, and I could easily see a group of patrolmen surmising that Baxter might have dropped the bag of money out the window before answering his car alarm.

The fence ended at the edge of the sidewalk, or at least it had until the police cut it loose and rolled it back a good ten yards to explore what it uncovered. The space between the back wall and the chain link was just wide enough to accommodate a thin man, if he sucked it in and slid along with his face or back to the wall. Although it was hard to say what had been caught in that space before the police freed it, judging from the trash accumulated along the remaining section of the fence it had probably been a foot-deep pile of garbage.

I was about to go back around to the parking lot when I noticed something inside the coil of fence which the police had tied off to the next post down. The rolled barrier was secured with yellow police tape, but I figured it was simply what had been on hand and not intended as a legitimate police line, not to be crossed. I untied it and discovered that ten yards of rolled chain link is both heavy and unwieldy. I struggled with the madly shifting metal tree trunk until remembering that I wanted it to unroll, and simply stepped back.

It fell sideways at first, hitting the motel wall and stopping to catch its breath before continuing to unwind. Its base slid toward me with three or four short hops, but then it came apart entirely and sagged to the pavement in full extension. This was fortunate, as I wasn't sure I could wrestle it up into its old position without help, and having identified the object I now wanted to learn its proximity to Baxter's back window.

The item was a combination padlock with a blue dial, and it had not been attached to the fence for long. If the chain link had been standing upright, the lock would have been about six inches off the ground directly under Baxter's window.

I wondered if the police had even noticed it, and decided it was time to ask them.

MY RECEPTION AT THE DAVIS police department was decidedly different when I was alone. Spears kept me waiting in the lobby for a good fifteen minutes, and I was struck by how much the Davis police station felt like a doctor's office. The lobby held ten vinyl chairs and a coffee table covered with magazines, but what most reminded me of a doctor's office was the quiet. Even the tiny station in Exile usually had some kind of activity, but there in Davis nothing ever seemed to be happening. In fact, if the man behind the desk were not wearing a badge and a uniform it would be hard to say just what kind of office this was at all.

After making me think I had been forgotten, the detectives finally summoned me down the back hall. Even this change of scenery did nothing to dispel the sense of crisp, organized lethargy, and when I walked into the detectives' room all three of them were there, seated behind desks that still remained remarkably bare.

"Whatcha need, Cole?" It was the kind of question that a busy man would ask while typing away at a report or poring over documents, but Spears was leaning back in his chair, jacket off, clearly in place for the next several hours.

I dropped into one of the chairs Winslow and I had used in the days before, and decided to shake things up a bit.

"Oh, anything you might have on Elijah Springer."

Spears did not even sit up straight upon hearing that, instead looking over either shoulder at his fellow detectives. Both Ramirez and Mayfair smirked at him, and he was downright rude when he looked back at me.

"Elijah Springer? I'm afraid you'll have to go to Mobile and ask the police there about him. Not exactly a resident of Davis."

"It's just that I would have thought he'd drop by here, as he drove through on the way to Exile yesterday. To see me."

That brought him to a full upright position, but not out of shock. He looked more like a guy trying to sneak up on a fly, but at least he wasn't smirking anymore.

"Elijah Springer came to see you?"

"Yeah, yesterday afternoon before I went to work at the cabstand…didn't he come see you as well?"

"Of course not. We've got no connection to the Springers at all," Spears snapped, and the other two began nodding like idiots.

"I see. A little different from the story the other day, but it does explain why no one is tailing Billy Lee. I would guess you guys talked to the D.A. and he told you to dummy up about the hot tip at the Seaview."

"There was a tip, but from a confidential informant who will remain nameless until the D.A. talks to the judge."

"And Billy Lee's shadow?"

"Couldn't spare the manpower."

I looked around the neat, uncluttered office and its silent phones.

"Yeah, your hands do seem full here, don't they?"

"So what did this Springer fellow have to say, Mr. Cole? You want to swear out a complaint?"

I ignored that. "You guys are kicking Dennis Sharp's murder into the dead letter file already?"

"Dead runaway, probably a drug deal gone bad, a couple of suspects who haven't been heard from in days, I think that one moved down the road," Mayfair recited from my left.

"The girl's still in the area, still actively trying to find out where Dennis Sharp went that night."

"She's his girlfriend. Why wouldn't she still be asking questions?" This from Ramirez on my right. I almost coughed up the new information about the note at the weigh station, along with other considerations which linked the girl to the other two suspects, but restrained myself at the last second. They were already covering their tracks, and so it was time to get what I'd come there for.

"Maybe so. And since the case seems dormant, I'd just like to tie up a couple of questions for the family."

"The family? You mean the convicted felons?"

"Still family. Anyway, I was out at the Seaview this morning and I spoke with somebody on the cleaning crew. Seems you guys tossed Baxter's motel room pretty hard that night. Was that because his car alarm was going off, or were you actually looking for something?"

They didn't like hearing about the car alarm again, but it reminded them that Winslow and I could still cause trouble with Baxter's case despite their united front with the D.A. Confidential informant or not, the

car alarm story was something they'd sooner forget, and
so Spears decided to throw me something.

"Everything went by the book there. We impounded
the car, conducted a thorough search of the room, and
then found the drugs in the car at the impound. The
C.I. told us that there would be money in the car, too,
so when we only found drugs we naturally assumed
the cash was in Baxter's room. So we radioed back
and had the police search the room and the surrounding grounds."

"So there was a bit of a break between the first thorough inspection and the second thorough inspection?"

"Don't get cute. We had the kid lock up the room and
posted a patrolman on it. We had uniforms all over that
parking lot until late that morning. Nothing happened
between the two inspections."

"The kid?" I'd become used to referring to Dennis
Sharp by that title.

"Yeah, the night clerk. He came out when we hit the
place, opened up Baxter's room for us, and locked it up
when we were done with the initial survey."

"The night clerk? Not Canfield, the manager?"

"Canfield wasn't there yet. The kid had to call him
from home, but we told him we weren't waiting and he
opened the door."

His supporting actors had fallen asleep on him, but
came awake with a vengeance at this point. Ramirez
led off.

"What are we talkin' to this guy for, Hank? He doesn't even have a license."

"Still checking up on a drug bust that went off three nights ago. You can always tell the amateurs," Mayfair remarked.

"We done here, Cole?" Spears actually looked about him for something to pick up and look at, but as I said the desks were pretty clean.

"Sure. Thanks for your help." I stood up slowly, letting them hope I was going to leave. "Hey, that bag of money? It ever turn up?"

"Never there."

I smiled, and Spears tried to give me the Davis equivalent of the Manny Batista Stare. It was a poor imitation.

"Elijah Springer mentioned it, is all. He seemed to think it was there." I turned toward the door, letting the implication blossom. This was yet another issue that might arise in Baxter's court case, and missing money can seriously sidetrack an otherwise solid prosecution.

"The guy's insane, Cole. Proven in court. Who's gonna listen to him?"

"Oh, nobody." I had the door open, and stepped through it with my parting line. "But I thought you said you didn't know him."

EXITING THE POLICE STATION into the midday heat, I began counting my blessings. I had gone there hoping to estab-lish the time frame between the initial search of Baxter's room and the real search some hours later, and had done that. Obviously the first walk-through had been little more than a cursory inspection, and so the police had assumed the money was hidden in the car along with the drugs. When that had turned out to be wrong they had started the real hunt, the search which had gone around back and peeled back the chain link.

I had to believe that Baxter had dropped the money out the back window of his room, and maybe even secured its container to the chain link with the combination lock. He'd been arrested moments later, the police had given his room the once-over, and the bag had been invisible amidst the garbage. It was likely that no one had even looked back there at first.

There was always the chance that one of the policemen had taken it, but I found that unlikely. No matter how much I see it in the movies, I do not believe that many cops are on the take or corrupt in any way. My fact-checking work had brought me into contact with quite a few of them over the past year, and my overall impression was that the vast majority of them are trying to follow the rules.

Besides, Dennis Sharp had been watching Baxter's room most of the evening and probably saw him bringing his bags in when he arrived. Knowing that the drug courier was also transporting money, he would have kept his eyes peeled for a smaller case so that he'd have a good idea if his car theft would also yield some cash. It was not impossible that he had seen Baxter being arrested and had taken a quick peek around the back of his room just in case something had been thrown out the room's window. As a con man imitating a runaway teen, Dennis was no doubt familiar with the various responses to police knocking at the door.

In the meantime there was the new wrinkle of the desk clerk at the Seaview. When I had spoken to Canfield, he had maintained that his assistant had been sitting the desk when Sharp ran by, and that he, Canfield, had been handling the police. With the cleaning lady's revelation about Canfield's extracurricular activities in mind, it was not hard to see where he might have been and why he might lie, but I had not known about the desk clerk's involvement in the drug bust. Until then, I had known of his role in giving Dennis Sharp a room, but that was it. Was it possible that he had taken the money bag? That he had somehow seen it while standing in Baxter's room with the police on their first check?

Perhaps there had been no money at all, as Spears believed. Perhaps Baxter had already dropped the package at its destination. Perhaps a guy walking his dog saw Baxter putting the bag outside the window in the presence of a whole lot of flashing police lights and had walked over to investigate. Perhaps. Maybe. Suppose.

The words spun around in my head, and I decided it was high time I got some sleep. Trying hard to keep my eyes open as I drove, I had to ponder the idea that Spears and his fellow detectives might be right, in an indifferent sort of way. Maybe the trail was indeed growing cold. Maybe this one had indeed gone down the road.

THE PHONE RANG LATE IN THE afternoon, and it was Winslow.

"Ain't you supposed to be at the cabstand by now?" he asked in a loud voice, and it sounded as if he were in an office somewhere.

"Now, isn't that the way it always is? Show up early for work a few times and they start thinking that's when your shift starts. I've got two more hours."

"Anything new?"

"Where are you?"

"We've got a little office here in Mobile, and I've been using it as a base of operations." He sounded upbeat, so I suspected he had something to tell me. "Never did get to talk with the Springers, but I did have an interesting talk with the local police."

"What did they have?" I had been up already, sorting through the various pictures and documents from the case so far, trying to see if any kind of inspiration popped up from the pile.

"Turns out that Dennis Sharp's arrest for traveler's check fraud was a little more involved than it sounded. It got knocked down to almost nothing because he gave a fake name and because the police couldn't really figure out what happened. Here's how it went.

"Sharp had come across some unsigned traveler's checks, about a hundred dollars' worth, but genuine.

He might have stolen them, but given the money he was depositing in the family accounts he probably bought them. He then made some reasonably good copies of the genuine checks, using the right kind of paper and a digital copier."

"That wouldn't provide a watermark."

"No, it wouldn't, and it wouldn't pass muster a couple of other ways, but I think Dennis was experimenting here. Here's how the rest went. He dresses up as a teenager, walks into a private travel agency, not one of the chain operations, and says his dad told him to cash in the remaining traveler's checks from the family vacation.

"He picked agencies that looked like they were riding the rims money-wise, and near as the police can tell he made them think they were taking him for a ride. He'd hand the agent an envelope containing one genuine check and the copies of a few others. They'd be in sequence because his originals had been in sequence, and here's the catch: Written on the envelope would be some number that was less than the amount of checks it contained.

"So if the number is 'sixty,' he'd hand the envelope over and ask if he could get sixty dollars for it. The agent takes out the first one, the genuine one, holds it up to the light, sees the watermark, and counts the remaining checks. That's when the agent sees that he's getting a hundred dollars in checks for sixty dollars, and says okay. It also gave him a reason not to take the remaining checks out and look at them."

"That worked?" I asked.

"Greed, Frank, greed. The grifters count on it. And even if the agent was suspicious, the wording of the request is important. 'Can I get sixty dollars for this?' could also mean the kid is holding hot checks and is basically trying to fence them. Judging from the number of phony checks that showed up in the weeks after Dennis skipped town, quite a few folks said yes. So instead of paying sixty dollars for a hundred dollars in checks, they paid sixty dollars for a single twenty-dollar check and four fakes."

"Amazing. So how did that get knocked down to almost nothing?"

"As usual, Dennis put on his homeless face and convinced the judge that he found the checks in the street and that it was a one-time thing. Remember, the other checks that he'd passed at the other shops were still being processed when he got caught, with serial numbers that matched the numbers of outstanding checks already purchased, and he'd given a fake name."

"Kid had nerves of steel."

"The kid had contempt for everyone around him, Frank. It doesn't take nerves of steel when you think you're running a game on morons. And let's not forget that he got caught.

"Anyway, it gets better. Since this was a much bigger case of fraud than the record indicated, I got on the phone to Miami to find out just what he'd done down there. This is where it gets interesting. He was through experimenting, and he'd gotten good enough at duplicating traveler's checks to forget about the travel agencies and hit the banks instead.

"He went on a real tear down there. They think he identified the cashiers in a few banks who weren't doing their jobs right. Maybe they just weren't trained, or they were lazy, but the police believe he cashed a few genuine traveler's checks just to see which cashiers were checking for the watermark, or even looking the checks over at all.

"So then he didn't have to worry about an envelope with a number written on it. When he got caught, he was passing five hundred dollars of checks and not one of them was genuine. He'd have gotten away with it, too, but the number exceeded the bank's limit for cashing traveler's checks without a manager's approval, you know, money laundering prevention, and the checks didn't hold up under the added scrutiny.

"They say he produced a fake ID, sat at the manager's desk for almost an hour, and didn't even try to run when they arrested him."

"You wanna talk about ice water now?" I remarked.

Winslow continued. "The funny part is that the fake ID held up until he posted bail. Over the next weeks, several thousand dollars' worth of those fake checks popped up, and the Miami cops think there might still be a lot more out there. They guess that he wasn't just hitting the banks, that he was working the airport, bars, casual grifter stuff with traveler's checks miraculously found on a stool between him and the mark. Greed, Frank. Gets people in trouble every time."

"I guess so. You think the girl was with him by then?"

"Hard to say, and I've been asking. A lot of the time a grifter will have a helper who's so smooth that nobody noticed him, so maybe she was with him the whole time. No one at either hearing remembers her, at least not from the photo, and it looks like Dennis used both his phone calls to arrange bail."

"But he didn't need bail in Mobile."

"Right, but he was fighting the clock in both Mobile and Miami. It'd be a heck of a thing if he fooled the judge and still got caught on a fingerprint match just because he hadn't already arranged the bond."

"Kid thought of everything."

"Not everything. He's still dead, remember? So what have you found while I been gone?"

Winslow already knew about the note at the weigh station, so I quickly ran through my discussion with the police and the discoveries at the Seaview. He was particularly impressed by the cleaning lady's revelations.

"Look, I'm not gonna be back until late tonight, so let's meet at that cabstand and compare notes. I'll call you when I'm getting close."

"Got it."

"Good job again, Frank, and you were right about the

Springers not seeing me. I needed to cool off before I could say that, but if I gave you a hard time I'm sorry."

"Forget it. I'll see you tonight."

"See you tonight."

TEN

THE PHONE RANG AGAIN A half hour later, and it was Beth Ann.

"Hey, tiger. Feel like getting a bite to eat before work?" It was a night when she did not teach class. Normally this would have been a nice phone call to receive, but I was getting somewhere with Gray's matrices and needed to beg off.

"I'm sorry, Beth Ann, but I'm still going through some of the papers from that drifter I told you about and I want to wrap that up before I go in." I figured this was a good explanation, as it was the truth and she had recommended my involvement in the first place.

Wrong again.

"Frank, how much longer are you going to keep this cabstand job?"

"I'm sorry, Beth Ann, but right now it's paying the bills." I ruminated darkly on girls I'd known who supported deadbeat boyfriends who never even looked for a job, but pushed that aside before it got me in trouble. Remembering something, I offered in a bright voice, "Hey, my old college buddy Mark is going to be here Saturday. I'd really like for you to meet him. What about we all go out to dinner then?"

Strike two.

"Frank, I really don't want to meet him." She paused, but it was just long enough to decide to lay out the cards. "How long are you going to play this game, Frank? Your life is passing you by, and your good buddy Mark is rooting you on. It's easy for him to tell you to stay the course—he's living it up in Manhattan, he's living his life, but where are you?"

I wasn't ready for this conversation, and despite its serious nature I found my eyes drifting back toward the pictures and other debris on my coffee table. Dennis Sharp was calling from that pile. A solution to the case was calling from that pile. Some modest, temporary resolution in a life gone upside down was calling from that pile.

"Hey, how about you come by the stand and we talk then?" I meant it, and I didn't want to lose Beth Ann, but I was not in any frame of mind to do this at the moment.

"I don't think so, Frank. Look, I don't want to say something I'm going to regret, so why don't we just leave things until after your friend has gone home? He's just down for the weekend, right?"

At least it wasn't a breakup, at least not yet, and it was a relief that she didn't want to pursue this topic. Not yet, anyway.

"That's probably a good idea. We are going to talk, aren't we?"

We both knew what that question meant, and she dropped the edge from her voice.

"Yes, we will, crazy man. You are crazy, you know that, right?"

"That makes us a good pair then."

"I guess it does, doesn't it?" There was a silence, and she ended the conversation. "Have fun with your old roommate, Frank. Call me when he's gone."

It was only after I'd returned to the documents that I remembered the office people scurrying by the cabstand late at night, whispering explanations into cell phones about why they weren't with the people who were important to them.

I BUNDLED UP MY VARIOUS pictures and paper grids and headed in to work a little later. Corelli had a good laugh when I told him the Davis police had never assigned anyone to watch Billy Lee, but then asked me not to tell the defenseless driver for fear that he might run off again. I tried to explain that Billy Lee's time on the bounding main had made his cab look awfully inviting, but Corelli was already out the door.

After the normal radio checks and disrespectful banter, I settled in with my various papers and tried to make sense of what I had. One of my biggest obstacles was the prevalence of outright lies in the things I had been told, and it really messed up parts of the grids which should have given me some answers. I would have to show this to Gray when next I saw him, and ask how his system worked if everybody lied.

Shoving the handwritten pages aside, I studied the

police bulletin about the fugitive Dennis Sharp and tried to align it with Winslow's description of events in Mobile and Miami. Winslow's trip west had not proven to be an absolute bust, as it had filled in some blanks about Dennis Sharp's criminal activities in the last months of his life. The new information supported my belief that Dennis had been retooling himself as a low-level confidence man, and that like any journeyman he had been taking his lumps while learning his trade.

There seemed to be a clear demarcation between Mobile and Miami, however, and using a fake name to get out of jail had something to do with it. He'd been comfortable enough giving his real name in Texas and Louisiana, but both of those arrests had been low caliber. Vagrancy and panhandling. Perhaps they had been slightly more serious than the record showed, as was the case with his arrest in Mobile, but they were still nickel-and-dime.

Even the traveler's check fraud in Mobile hadn't been sophisticated enough to be called anything better than simple grifting. His targets had been small, independent travel agencies with larcenous employees, and even then it had not been for big money. Regardless, he had used his considerable acting skills when arrested on that one, and just to keep his previous arrests from jacking up his bail or preventing his release entirely.

But why? He had access to a fair amount of money in the family account, and even linked to the same Dennis Sharp arrested for vagrancy and panhandling he would not have been denied bail. By giving his fake identity to the police he had made extra trouble for himself, and by running off he had made himself a fugitive.

Mobile certainly seemed to have been a departure point for him, because the Dennis Sharp who surfaced in Miami was no longer confining himself to low-level crime. He was passing counterfeit traveler's checks in various banks, and doing so in amounts which tripped anti-money-laundering alarms. I could not see him walking up to a bank teller dressed as a runaway, either, so the odds were good that he'd been decked out in suit and tie and acting his age. So what had changed his game plan, and what had changed it back by the time he came to the Panhandle?

The answer to both questions was the same: The Springers. It was just too big a coincidence that the first place he'd given a fake name to the police was also the hometown of the gang which had eventually dogged his footsteps. I did not know what he had done to bother the Springers, but the tape he left for his parents identified the gang as his new employers, and I had to assume his transgression had been major.

Or had it? Maybe his trick with the traveler's checks had been enough all by itself to set off Uncle Elijah and the rest of the family. Maybe he'd unwittingly selected a tiny one-horse travel agency which was also a front for some other Springer enterprise, and so had incurred the family's wrath. If that was the case, his eagerness to get out of police custody and then out of town would make sense. And if he'd been visited in the lockup by a Springer lawyer, he might have realized that his trip out of town should involve a more lucrative kind of con game.

Hence the trip to Miami and the check fraud with the banks. He'd become a fugitive and locked horns with the federal government because he was in much more serious trouble with a far more lethal opponent. No wonder he'd been cool as a cucumber when being arrested in Miami. With his traveler's check game gone, he had little choice but to contact the gang in Mobile and find out what they felt would make things right.

All roads, it seemed, led back to the Seaview. The Springers had assigned him the relatively lowball task of stealing the drug car, and he had switched back into the role of a runaway. Perhaps the girl's presence had something to do with that, and not for the first time did I wish I knew more about her. When had they hooked up? Was she a legitimate runaway, or were they peas of the same pod?

At any rate, Dennis had slipped back into his earlier character, but not quite. Perhaps the jaunt in Miami had reminded him of a better life, or perhaps he was just sick of sleeping in the gutter, but he'd made a decision that still struck me as a mistake. He'd rented a room. Granted, it was with a stolen credit card and, of necessity, a phony name, but it was still an odd risk to take.

I rummaged through my papers and came up with the copy of the credit card receipt, the impression of

the stolen card taken on the night in question. Once
again I had to admire the kid's skills, and his nerve. He
had not known that the Seaview's credit card validation
machine frequently malfunctioned, and even if he did,
there was no guarantee it would happen that night. No,
he'd been ready with some insanely complicated tale
of a munificent uncle loaning him the card for a little
fun in the sun in Florida, and no doubt it would have
worked.

Holding the receipt up to the light, my eyes fixed on
something truly out of place. The card's expiration was
more than a year past. The slickest con man would have
a hard time getting around that little glitch, and it was
a miracle that the Seaview's machine had been out of
whack that night. What was it that the manager, Canfield, had said about that? They did not need the actual
card to make a second attempt at a credit check, and
would have simply typed in the number if they'd tried
again later.

If they'd tried again later. According to the Davis police, the only individual who might have tried that was
the kid behind the desk, the same one who accepted
Denis Sharp's crazy story in the first place. The one
who'd been so concerned with the chance of that particular guest skipping out on his bill that he'd kept a
weather eye out for him. He'd put him in the room directly over his head just in case, and yet he hadn't tried
the card a second time.

Visions of conspiracy flashed before my eyes. Just

how lucky could Dennis Sharp have been? To get a break from the credit check machine, to get a room facing the car he was going to steal, and then to get another break on his stolen credit card when the kid failed to try it again?

My mind went back to the Seaview that morning, particularly to the back window of Baxter's room. According to Spears, the kid from the desk had let the police into the room for their first, desultory check of the premises. Had he seen the bag, and tipped Dennis off? Had he been allowed in the room, maybe just long enough to make sure the back window was unlocked? Had he stood by the window and seen the money bag outside, locked to the fence?

The fact that I had never laid eyes on this phantom reception jockey brought me back, but not far. Looking at the receipt again, I knew one thing: The tale about Dennis renting a motel room was actually as wrong as it had always sounded. And there was only one way to get to the bottom of it.

I had managed the taxi dispatcher's duties from behind the wheel of a Midnight cab only once before, but that had been an emergency and this was not. I was not sure just how Corelli would react to this, but I had to go to the Seaview while that kid was still riding the desk. Forwarding the cabstand phone to my cell, I locked up and headed for one of the spare rigs. Turning on the car's radio, I got a good check with each of the drivers out that night, and then got on the road.

THE TWO TIMES THAT I TOOK the dispatch job on the road actually worked out quite well, and left me wondering just why I had to sit in that boring cabstand all night. The first time had involved dealing with customers, and while this had somewhat complicated matters it had not stymied me, and it had not turned the evening into a nightmare. With a little help from the other cabbies I had found my way from Point A to Point B, and I hadn't missed a call or failed to log an entry the entire night.

The second time was the night I went out to ask a few questions at the Seaview, and even though I was concerned about losing my job I still feel that the taxi part of the evening went off without a hitch. I suppose it was easier this time because I had done it before and was not dealing with customers, but I would still have to hand my duties off to Ruby when I went inside the motel office, and a lot could go wrong with that.

I even tackled a call as I drove, nimbly typing the required information into the personal assistant taped to the dash before assigning the fare to Tony. I had brought the cabstand map board with me, and discovered that I hadn't needed to look at it to know that Tony was the closest rig and had no passengers at the time.

With that done, I began mentally preparing for my interview with the desk clerk. It occurred to me that Canfield might be behind the desk, as he would have to be a man of superhuman endurance to be gone alley-catting every single night, but even that would have its purpose. Canfield believed his assistant had been hoodwinked by Sharp, and when I showed him the expiration date on that credit card receipt he was likely to spill something.

And if he tried to be a tough guy I could always ask him where he had been for at least the first part of the festivities the night the police arrested Baxter.

I almost drove straight into the motel parking lot, but as I was piloting a mustard-colored taxi bearing the Midnight emblem I decided to put the rig somewhere inconspicuous. There was a quiet strip mall across the street, and I put the taxi behind a parked delivery truck before gathering my evidence and jogging across the darkened street.

It was still hot out, and the air-conditioner which serviced the motel office was humming loudly as I went by. I got ready to see Canfield behind the counter, and went through the door.

A tall, impossibly thin teenager looked up at me from behind the counter, and I stopped short in the doorway. He was probably twenty, with blue eyes the color of powdered detergent. His close-cropped hair was blond, but the mustache and goatee were dark brown and for an instant I tried to guess which one was dyed. His eyes were big, but his nose was small and I think that was what gave him the permanent look of a smart aleck. I disliked him on the spot.

"Hi, you Canfield's assistant?"

"Who wants to know?"

I didn't really have a lot of time to do this. I had to

be physically located at the cabstand to re-forward the phone to Ruby or one of the others, so at any moment my cell phone could go off and I would have to answer it.

Coming straight up to the desk, I pulled the police sketch from the folder and dropped it in front of him. I meant this as an icebreaker, as my real intent was to see his reaction to a picture of Dennis Sharp.

"Recognize these two?" I asked in my best cop voice.

"Sure. Two more rent-a-cops like you, asking questions about the drug bust a few nights ago." He snorted this time, letting the amusement show. "Day late and a dollar short. So what are you, their boss? Trying to find your boys?"

"Actually, they weren't in here asking about the drug bust." I tried hard not to let my voice tremble. Something about this guy really got under my skin, and I was in danger of starting to trip over my words. "They were asking about this guy here."

I had meant to surprise him with the large mug shot of Dennis Sharp, but fumbled with the papers and came up with the picture showing Dennis and Sally Hayes pressed up against each other in the photo booth. I looked down just in time to see what it was, decided it was good enough, and dropped the picture of the happy couple onto the counter.

You could say that I won this round, as the wise guy suddenly looked like he'd eaten something that had disagreed with him. His leering face went taut, and he was momentarily transfixed by the paper in front of him.

I had not expected that reaction. I had planned to show him the picture, get him to acknowledge that he knew Dennis Sharp, find out if he knew him as Sharp or Taylor, and then rake him over the coals for getting taken by a teen runaway. Somewhere in the middle of that I was going to introduce the credit card receipt, get the truth out of him about the room that Sharp allegedly rented, and then go for the knockout by asking where the money was.

Luckily, the kid's sneering insouciance had made me so mad that I had already lost my train of thought when I saw his reaction to the photo. With all my prepared lines gone, I said the first thing that came to mind.

"Something wrong, son?"

I watched his face try to get back into its normal hostile stance while his brain raced for an answer. It came to him only half-formed, and came out the same way.

"Naw, nothing. It's just that the girl is really hot. Don'tcha think so?" He was trying to include me in the gang now, and I would have agreed with his appraisal of Sally Hayes if I thought the picture did her justice. It was a copy of the photo booth printout, and even though it was a fair duplicate I felt the original was nothing to write home about.

That was what told me that the picture of Dennis was not the thing which had upset his digestion. It was the girl's image which surprised him, and I also detected a hint of jealousy at seeing her so chummy with the run-away from a few nights before. He was reacting this way because he'd already met her.

"She sure is. But you've met her before. Right?"

He was completely rocked back on his heels by that one, and it was with intense enjoyment that I heard him start to sputter.

"Her? No, what made you think…I've never seen her before."

"Sure?"

"What are you saying?" He had finally become so flustered that he'd come all the way back around to mindless hostility, and for a moment I thought he might take a swing at me. I was on a roll, though, and so I tapped the picture with my index finger.

"See the guy in this picture? What's his name again?" I'd read this trick in a detective book, where the interviewer pretends to forget the name of a man whom the suspect claims not to know.

"Dennis Taylor." His eyes jumped. "At least that's the name he gave me."

"Yeah, well, he's dead." I let the words sink in before continuing. "Somebody shot him in the chest at point-blank range. And the girl's mixed up in it. You sure you never met her?"

"I'm not talking to you anymore." He was looking around him, trying to evade eye contact. "In fact, get out. You're not a cop, and if you aren't gone in ten seconds I'm going to call one."

I gave him the Manny Batista Stare until he looked away again, and then I began slowly gathering my papers.

"Sure. When did you say Canfield's due back?"

"I didn't."

"That's okay. If you see him, tell him I'll be back." I held up the folder as if it contained the key to success in life. "And if that hot little number comes by here, like I think she already has, you better get on the horn to the police right away. They want to talk to her about her boyfriend. The dead guy. Get it?"

I walked out without waiting for an answer, and was across the street before realizing I hadn't even gotten his name.

ELEVEN

SOME OF THE P.I.'s I HAVE met have mentioned scenes like this one, where they had gone in with a set of questions about a certain piece of information and come away with something completely different. At first I felt giddy, seeing that the entire revelation had been caused by the purely accidental selection of the photo booth picture, but as I walked toward the cab the feeling approached euphoria.

So Sally had given up on the idea that the boys at the Midnight Service could help her, and had done what I had done. She'd come back to the motel itself, the scene of the crime, and started piecing it together from there. Doing a little chronological calculation, I had to suspect that she had come to this conclusion well before I did, but then again she hadn't been handicapped by trips to the Davis police department and visits from elderly members of the Springer gang.

The real question now involved whether or not the kid at the desk had told her about taking the money. This seemed unlikely, considering that this was a girl who had shot her own boyfriend before getting him to tell her where the loot was stashed. If she had finally solved the puzzle, she'd have done whatever was necessary to recover the cash.

If the desk clerk had not yet told her about the money, then the odds were good that Sally would be by to exert a little more pressure. She might even bring her two buddies, and I was in a unique position to witness this. Thinking it through, I got an absolute thrill when I considered the possibility that the jerk behind the desk had dialed her number as soon as I left.

My mind was moving quickly, but in a thorough, organized fashion. First, I had to reposition the cab so that I could see through the office window without being noticed. Second, I had to get Winslow on the phone, hopefully to learn that he was on the outskirts of town and could join me for the vigil. Third, I had to notify the rest of the Midnight cabbies that I was out of the booth. I had not bothered to do that because I had expected the trip to the Seaview to be brief.

In case the kid was watching, I fired up the taxi and drove off back down the road in the direction of Davis proper. Cutting back through a side street, I pulled around the back of the strip mall and parked near the end of the elongated building. Walking hunched over like a commando in a movie, I rounded the corner and saw that I would be able to see into the motel office from there. It looked shadowy enough for me to take a chance, so I moved the cab forward just enough and killed the engine.

Roughly two hundred yards away, the clerk was visible in the light of the office window. He had the phone in his hand, and I crossed my fingers in the mad hope that my inadvertent brilliance would yield up the girl.

Reaching for the cell phone, I hesitated for a second. I had been lucky so far, as it was a quiet night and there had been few calls for Midnight taxis. This did not mean we had no fares, as Ruby and the others knew where to cruise to catch the late-night partygoers, but it did mean that I might miss a call while speaking with Winslow.

Well, whoever wanted a cab would have to wait five minutes and call back. I dialed Winslow's number and he picked up after the first ring.

"Hey, Frank, what's up?"

"Listen, I can't talk long. I'm in a taxi parked across the street from the Seaview Motel. I'm next to a coin-op laundry, and I'm watching the desk clerk. I think he's been in touch with Sally Hayes and that she may even be by here tonight. How fast can you get here?"

"Pretty fast. I'm just outside of Panama City. Can you tell me what put you onto this?"

"I think the desk clerk swiped the money Baxter was carrying. He let the police in to search the room, but according to Spears they didn't do a very thorough job the first time. So either the bag was thrown out the window or it was still in the room when they locked it up and put a guard on it. Anyway, I think the desk clerk got hold of it."

Winslow probably didn't get much of that, but he could tell I was lathered up and that was good enough.

"Okay, we'll talk when I get there. I'll be on foot, so don't get surprised when I come up on you. And Frank—"

"Yeah."

"If she does show up, call the cops. Don't do anything stupid here. All we want is Dennis Sharp's killer behind bars. No heroics. Got it?"

I honestly didn't know what he was talking about. That is, until about forty-five minutes later.

THE CABBIES FIGURED OUT I wasn't in the booth, and because I had not told them of my relocation they decided to have some fun with me. It started with the normally quiet Danny Parsons, which explains why I didn't pick up on it more quickly.

"Base, this is Danny."

"Go ahead, Danny."

"Frank, I've got a little problem. I've been asked to go to a Magnolia Avenue in Bending Palms, but I don't know where that is."

This was a problem. Back at the booth I would have punched up the address on the internet, but I was not at the booth. I had the map board with me, and had been updating the drivers' locations with colored pushpins, but finding an unfamiliar street on it would require close scrutiny. It would also force me to turn on the overhead light and risk giving away my position.

"Anybody? Anybody know where Magnolia Avenue is in Bending Palms?" I took the lazy man's way out and broadcast the request to all of the drivers.

There was dead silence, and I began fumbling in the glove compartment for a flashlight. Even that was going to be risky, and I had no idea if I was going to be able to read the tiny print on the board while basically lying on top of it. It was a large piece of plywood that took up most of the passenger side of the front seat, and I had to find Magnolia Avenue in the index before locating it on the map. Just as I began searching with the flashlight pressed against the map, Danny came back on.

"Frank, could you hurry? My fare's getting pretty excited."

There were a number of ways that a fare might not know the location where he was headed, but hopefully not at one in the morning. Magnolia Avenue sounded like a residential area, and I straightened up long enough to get the microphone.

"Uh, Danny, is your fare by any chance going home?"

"I think so, Frank."

Now it was my turn to provide the silence. Peering around the steering wheel to make sure the kid at the motel desk was still there, I waited for Danny to let me off the hook. He didn't, and after a minute I called him back.

"Danny, does your fare know where his house is?"

"I bet he does, Frank, but I can't ask him."

"Is your fare unconscious?"

"Oh, no, very awake, Frank, it's just that he's…" The voice trailed off, and I began hearing the sounds of a man and a woman having a good time in the back of Danny's van. "I really don't want to disturb him."

This kind of thing was against company rules, but I had already run into too much opposition trying to enforce Corelli's regulations and did not want to go down that road again.

"Well, did they give you an idea where the address is?"

There was a long pause, and when Danny's mike came back on it sounded as if the couple in the back had been joined by others.

"Frank? Frank? I'm gonna need some guidance here. They're asking me to pull over and get in the back with them. Am I supposed to do that?"

The commotion in the back of his van reached a crescendo at that point, and somewhere in the midst of the sounds I recognized the audio track from a famous risqué film. The microphone came alive as well, with the simultaneous voices of Tony, Billy Lee, and Ruby.

"Tell him to go for it, Frank!"

"Pictures, Danny! Pictures!"

"If that Midnight van's a-rockin'…"

And then all four of them were laughing uproariously over the radio. It was Manny's night off, or it would have been five. It took some time for the commotion to end, and Ruby came on.

"I can't believe you fell for that."

"Thanks, Rube. I really needed that aggravation right now."

"Where you at, Frank? Danny rolled by the booth but you weren't there. He said your rig was gone, too."

"I had to go over to West Davis. It's something connected to Billy Lee's fare a few nights ago."

"The dead guy?"

"Yeah."

"Well, he won't hear it from me, Frank, but if Corelli finds out he's not going to be happy."

"I know. I won't be out here much longer."

"Well, you be careful out there, cowboy. West Davis ain't the safest place to be, this time of night."

"Thanks."

I would have continued the conversation, but across the street Sally Hayes stepped through a back door in the Seaview's office and approached the desk clerk from behind. In one feline swoop she wrapped her arms around his chest, and although it was a distance, I think she was kissing his ear.

He did not seem surprised, but he did try to turn around as if he had something to say. Probably telling her about my visit, I would suppose, and now it occurred to me that my little drop-in might not have been all that good a thing after all. I was watching the office from across the street with no Winslow in sight, and now the two lovebirds had every reason to run out the back door with the loot.

That's what I mean by finding out what Winslow was trying to tell me. I went to call the police, but my cell phone had been knocked on the floor of the cab during my gymnastics with the map board and I couldn't find it. My eyes were fixed on the two young people across the way while I felt around for the phone, but the search got postponed right about then. He must have told her something she liked, because she suddenly jumped in the air, got her arms around his neck, and planted a big one on him. He reciprocated, and it didn't take a degree in nuclear science to know that he had revealed the truth about Baxter's money.

He probably agreed to go away with her, too, and since that meant I was watching a guy planning his own murder, I knew I had to do something. Forgetting the phone, I jumped out of the car and did the only thing I could do. I ran across the street and into the office.

I HIT THE DOOR PRETTY HARD, and it crashed against the wall as I went through. They were still in a clinch when I got there, so I got to feel relief, embarrassment, and even a little jealousy all at once. He was quite startled, and almost broke loose, but she remained composed, kept her grip, and simply rested her head on his chest while fixing me with a triumphant smile. She was wearing a white cotton top, bare at the midriff, over the pink sweatpants I'd seen two nights before. When she spoke, it was with a little girl's voice.

"Why, hi, Frank. What brings you here?"

"You know this guy?" the clerk asked, regarding me like an alien life-form.

"Of course I do. Frank's been a perfect dear. He was trying so hard to get me to talk with the police, and he just couldn't understand why I didn't want to do that."

The clerk's face screwed up a little, and he tried to assimilate her comments, but he only got far enough to ask, "Huh?"

"See what I was talking about, kid?" I asked, still near the door and wondering if I could get through it if she came up with a gun. "She's playing you. What did you two just decide? Just before I came in? Run away together with the money?"

"None of your business, guy. Now, I told you to get out—"

"Oh, don't be that way." Sally let go of him and leaned both her elbows on the counter. "Frank just can't get it through his head that it's over between us. That's why he's been following me. That's why he told you whatever he told you."

She had his buttons pretty well figured out. He fixed me with a look that male rams see on the face of the guy who's just about to head butt them.

"I only told him about Dennis, Sally. Why don't you tell him what happened to Dennis?"

"Dennis?" She was perfect. "I haven't seen Dennis in days. I think he went back to Texas, or wherever he was from."

"Drop the act, Sally. He knows Dennis is dead."

"No, I don't. You told me he was dead. You think I believe a word—"

I interrupted him. "So what happened, Sally? Were you mad that Dennis came back empty-handed? You were waiting at his campground, and when he showed up with nothing, you up and shot him."

The blue eyes were turned on full blast, but the corners of her lips gave her away. She was enjoying the memory, even though she chose her words carefully.

"He betrayed me. That's why we're not together."

The boy took a step back from her, sensing something sinister and beginning to reconsider his travel plans.

"*He* betrayed *you?* You cooked up a phony kidnapping, made it sound like the Springers snatched you for insurance, and now you say *he* betrayed *you?* And what exactly were your two buddies going to do to Dennis once he delivered the car, if this had gone off right?"

"Nothing. They were going to tell him where to find me, but I wasn't going to be there. I would have vanished, just like I'm going to do now."

The clerk noticed that he was no longer on the itinerary, and took another step farther away. As for me, I couldn't believe that a motel lobby could stay this empty this long, even at one in the morning. Don't people run out of ice anymore?

"So you let yourself get carried away, and you killed poor Dennis before finding out if he had managed to steal part of the loot." I turned to the boy, hoping to en-

ergize him. He was on the right side of the counter to
tackle her, and I was trying to save his life, so I felt he
owed me.

"Get it? Those two guys who came by asking about
Dennis weren't bail bondsmen. That's why they asked
if he was carrying anything when he ran off. You see,
their blonde friend here killed the kid before finding
out if he'd come away with anything."

"But, how would they know?" he asked in a per-
plexed, dazed sort of voice. I finally saw that he really
wasn't keeping up with the conversation, and that he
wasn't too bright to begin with. "I only found that bag
by accident—"

"When you went around to the back window." He
gave me a look of denial, but I was ready for that. "You
let the cops into Baxter's room the first time they went
looking. You saw something you liked, so you decided
to sneak around back after they'd locked the room up."

"Hey, it was just a Rolex! I saw it on the night table
and the guy didn't look like he'd be needing it, all the
cops he had around him. Looked like he was going to
jail for a thousand years. So I had a quick look around
once I climbed in the window, and that's when I found
the bag. I didn't know it was there, so how did those
other two?"

Now it was my turn to lose the thread of the dis-
course. My brilliant clue, the combination lock on the
chain-link fence, had been overlooked by the cops because it was nothing more than a discarded piece of

hardware. The clerk had gone in to steal Baxter's watch and, with a police guard making sure no one interrupted him, proceeded to ransack the room. Baxter had not put the bag outside, or locked it to the fence for safe-keeping, and the clerk had only opened it to see what it contained. I could imagine his eyes bugging out when he saw the loot, and that visual brought me back.

"It was a setup, kid. Dennis, Blondie here, her two buddies, even a few more people, they all knew what was in that car. Drugs and money. And when the money wasn't mentioned on the news, they started asking people like you and me if Dennis was carrying anything when he took that cab ride. They thought he might have got the money and stashed it.

"But when they were pretty sure he wasn't carrying anything when he left here, they finally zeroed in on you and Canfield. Canfield couldn't have done it because he wasn't here at first, so that left you."

"Shut up, Frank," Sally murmured, unconcerned, warning a toddler that the light socket was going to shock him, but willing to let it happen for sake of the lesson.

"So how did it go? She came in here with a sob story about the two guys in the sketch? Dennis owed them money, and so now they were leaning on her? She had to find the cash, and you were her only hope?" The clerk was staring at her hard by now. "Don't kick yourself too hard, kid. I fell for it, too."

"Told you to shut up, Frank." Sally's voice was no

longer playful, and I was suddenly grateful that the counter was between me and whatever retribution she had in mind. She was just on the verge of action, the muscles beneath the cotton top tightening, when the office door opened loudly. I turned, hoping to see the face of Curt Winslow but expecting to see some frazzled traveler looking for a room, and was wrong on both counts.

The two bail guys were standing there, and one of them had a gun.

"WELL, HELLO THERE, SALLY," said the one with the gun. Harry Ames, if I remembered correctly.

"Or whoever you are. There doesn't seem to be a Sally Hayes anywhere we looked," observed the tall one, Mark Knight.

"All right, let's get this show on the road. We're all going to step into the back room there." Ames turned and pointed the gun at me. It was an automatic that looked like it could tear great big holes in bank vault doors. "You first, Cole."

I started toward the counter, but stopped when I saw the girl's face. For the first time since I had known her, Sally looked like someone backed into a corner. She had been poised to do something physical just a moment before, and the arrival of her former partners did nothing to change that. Stepping back so that she was no longer within arm's reach of the kid, she came up with a snub-nosed revolver from heaven knows where.

Time slowed down a lot just then, but the funny part was the absence of shouting. Somehow I would have expected the people actually holding the guns to start screaming at each other, and it would not have been altogether unreasonable to expect the innocent bystanders to start in as well. Regardless of my expectations, Sally simply stood there with her elbow tucked in at her side and the gun held nice and level, and Ames and Knight hardly reacted at all.

"Gonna shoot us, Sal? Just like your boyfriend?" Ames's face was hard and featureless, but his tone was quiet, almost sympathetic. I got the impression he'd been in scenes like this before, and was not eager to upset the girl with the gun.

"I didn't shoot anybody." She said it deadpan, and for the briefest instant I almost believed it. "Now I'm going to take this bag here and go out the back. Anyone who follows me is going to get hurt."

She dipped her eyes toward the counter when she mentioned the money bag, and for the first time I became aware that Baxter's bag was tucked beneath the counter on the other side. That was what had made her so happy when she'd thought she was alone with the clerk. The guy was so stupid that he'd actually been waiting for her with the money sitting there for the taking.

"I've got a better idea." Ames had taken over the talking for his side of the room, and Knight let him. "You got me and my partner tangled up in a murder rap, honey, so I'd say that forfeits your cut of the proceeds. So why don't you just go out the back way and forget we ever met?"

I was not sure what that was going to mean for me and the other innocent bystander, but it seemed that Ames wanted to get at least one of the guns to leave the room.

"Leaving the money," Ames added.

Judging from Sally's expression, that was not about to happen. There was a long, brittle instant there when I thought the gunplay was about to start, and maybe it was, but the door opened somewhere in the middle of that.

A big man backed in, pushing the door open with his butt while trying to control a large bundle of news-papers on his left shoulder.

"Papers!" he announced gruffly, and just before he made his move I saw that it was Winslow.

Maybe this is something that Detroit cops learn, and maybe he just got lucky, but he brought his right hand up under the bundle and used it to slam the papers straight into Knight's head. The tall man dropped like a stone, and Winslow was already reaching for Ames before Knight reached the floor. He grabbed Ames's gun with both palms, his right shoulder was pressed up against Ames's front, and rammed the smaller man back against the wall with considerable force.

The gun popped loose after two tries, and Winslow came up with it just as Sally reached for the bag under the counter. This brought her gun hand near enough for me to imitate Winslow, and I grabbed her wrist with all my might. The kid behind the counter was of absolutely no use, standing there waiting to soak up some lead, and then I learned why it is a bad idea to reach for a gun this way.

She pumped at least two bullets straight into the outside wall, the explosions like cracks of thunder in my ears. I was still straining away at her arm, slowly pulling her over the counter, when Winslow stepped up from behind and obligingly kicked my legs out from under me. My insubstantial weight was still good enough to make her decide whether to keep the gun or have her arm broken, and I fell to the ground, along with the revolver.

"Don't touch it, Frank!" Winslow announced loudly, correctly guessing that my hearing was no longer one hundred percent with the gunshots still ringing in my ear. He reached over the counter and grabbed a fistful of that pretty blond hair. "Something tells me that's the gun that killed Dennis Sharp."

She began clawing at his arm, so Winslow dragged her up onto the desk to face the floor. Her arms kept flailing, but he stepped back out of reach and turned to her newest ex-boyfriend.

"Hey, buddy, how about calling the cops?"

You could say it was a full truckload when the police finally hauled everybody away. They actually left in several cars, but all told it was Ames and Knight, Sally, and the sneak thief from behind the front desk. I never did get his name.

Ames and Knight began singing long before the cops took them away, fully aware that they were accessories to a murder and seeing no reason to give Sally a chance to work her magic. The kid also began talking, somehow believing that climbing into a locked motel room to steal a guest's Rolex watch was mitigation for then stealing a bag containing a very large amount of cash from that same room. Sally kept her mouth shut, her face already worked up into that helpless, defeated runaway act, and were it not for the murder weapon in her possession I think it might just have worked.

Spears, Mayfair, and Ramirez were beside themselves with gratitude. It seems that the station actually could find them after normal duty hours when the circumstances warranted it, and they were down at the Seaview in no time.

Winslow arranged a meeting the next day to secure the necessary documents proving that Sally Hayes was in custody and was believed to be the murderer of Dennis Sharp, as he would need those to get paid.

Gray Toliver actually whooped with joy when I called to tell him what had happened, and we arranged to meet for a few games of chess the next morning.

And Corelli fired me for leaving my post.

TWELVE

"FRANK, I'M NOT DOUBTING your story, but how did your friend Winslow knock someone unconscious with a bundle of newspapers?" Gray asked, moving a chess piece on the concrete board between us. We were at the Exile public beach where we normally played, and I was trying to tie all the ends together for him.

"Well, it wasn't all newspaper." I moved a piece as well, but the game was not up to our usual performances. The story of the wayward Dennis Sharp was far too compelling for that. "It was more like a cinder block with newspapers wrapped around it."

"They teach that kind of thing in detective school?"

"I suspect he picked that up somewhere else."

Gray looked at the board, exhaled loudly, and tipped over his king even though the game's outcome was still very much in doubt.

"I can't concentrate. You know, you and I spent a lot of time putting all the facts of this case into nice, organized tables. Every place I've worked, that's how we kept things straight. And every time I've organized facts that way, the grids showed what didn't fit. What happened before it was supposed to. Which system was saying everything was all right when all the other systems said it wasn't. So what happened?"

"Well, Gray, the matrices did show us who knew Dennis as Sharp, and who knew him as Taylor. That alone was huge, because it showed the link between Sally and the two bail guys."

"But it didn't. They weren't really together."

"At the beginning they were. One of the odd things about the bail guys is that they told the truth about where they were from. They said they were chasing down a bail jumper, but their story about being from Mobile didn't fit because Dennis didn't post bail in Alabama. He posted it in Miami. So Winslow figured the bail guys were saying they were from Mobile because they knew the town and wouldn't get tripped up by basic questions about the place.

"While he was over in Mobile, Winslow had some of his firm's people hand out the police sketch of Ames and Knight, and it wasn't long before someone recognized them. They were never licensed bail bondsmen, bounty hunters, or anything like that, but they did track down strays for a bail agency that is now out of business.

"A few phone calls later Winslow's people found a secretary who used to work at that agency, and she recognized the picture of Sally Hayes. She couldn't come up with the specifics, and she didn't recognize Dennis Sharp, but it doesn't matter. Odds are that Sally met these two guys at that time and kept their phone number handy."

"Just called them up and asked them to kidnap her?"

"That bail agency's been out of business for over a year, so I bet this wasn't the first time they'd worked together. And remember, it was a fake kidnapping. Ames and Knight are definitely on the shady side, but they weren't putting on an act the first night I met them, when they denied claiming to be bounty hunters. They know where the fine line of the law falls, and when they realized Sally had murdered Dennis, they knew they were much further over the line than they were used to."

"So why didn't they just go home?"

"The money. They knew it hadn't been recovered, and they wanted to get what they came for. My guess is that Sally first called them up when Dennis told her about the car heist, and then had them call Dennis as he was headed to the motel. They told him they were working with the Springers, that there was a change in plan, and that they'd snatched his girlfriend just to make sure he wouldn't drive off with the car and the loot. They told him to go to the weigh station for further instructions once he had the car, and so that's what he did when the cops showed up at the Seaview. He didn't have the car or the money, he already suspected he was going to be murdered anyway—"

"He said that on the tape to his parents."

"Yes. So in a way, Sally and her friends did themselves in by saying they were with the Springers. At any rate, Dennis figured he was going to be murdered and decided to run for it."

"Leaving Sally in the lurch."

"That's the part I haven't quite got straight. He went back to his campsite to get his things, and that's where she killed him, but I can't imagine she was sitting there while her two buddies were supposed to be collecting the car and the loot. If I were her, I'd be in the shadows when Dennis made the exchange, and ride off into the sunset with my two new partners. So there had to be a lag time, a few hours when they were just waiting—"

"Unless they were watching the motel, too," Gray said. "Maybe they planned to watch Dennis steal the car, tail him to the weigh station, and then meet him at that strip mall. If that was the case, they'd know he skipped. They would have seen the police at the Seaview, tailed him to the message drop, and seen the cab drop him at the boardwalk."

I didn't think this was likely, but it was important to say this the right way. Gray was an awfully smart guy, as well as the first stranger to show me friendship when I first came to town, and it was easy to hurt his feelings if you made him feel stupid.

"I thought of that, but that's where the grids you worked up helped out. Remember, I had a lot of hours at the cabstand to go over this. Anyway, if they'd tailed him from the motel they'd have known he ran out of there empty-handed. Most of their work after that night

revolved around whether or not he was carrying anything, so it's unlikely they were watching him then. In
the meantime, if they'd been watching they might even
have gotten a good look at Billy Lee, but their search
always sounded like they had no idea who had driven
the cab."

"Okay, that makes sense." Gray's eyes got unfocused,
and I was afraid I'd insulted him anyway, but he was
only thinking. "Frank, can I have those grids back when
you're done with them? I want to work through this
again, see where it went wrong."

"Uh, I can't do that, Gray. Winslow asked for everything. He called it 'work product' or something like
that, and I got the impression it belongs to his firm."

"Oh."

"Besides, I can tell you where the system failed
us. Everybody involved in this was lying, or double-
crossing somebody. Who would have thought that the
clerk on the motel desk would see a Rolex watch on
Baxter's night table and decide to circle back and steal
it?"

"He probably did something like that a few times
before."

"Yeah, and he still thinks that it's an excuse to say
that he was only stealing the watch and happened to
stumble on the money."

"If he hadn't gone in there, the police would have
found that money and the whole thing would have been
over," Gray said.

"Exactly. Except let's not forget that the double-crossing started long before that. The Springers told Dennis his debts with the house would be settled if he stole the car, but then they set him up with the Davis police. And if the Davis police had followed instructions, they would have been waiting for Dennis at that highway rest stop instead of jumping the gun at the Seaview."

"You know, from what you've told me, these detectives are pretty much the Keystone Cops, but if they'd waited like they were told, they would have looked like fools. Dennis would have stolen that car, delivered it to the bail guys at that strip mall, and never gone near that rest stop. By jumping the gun, at least the Davis cops got what they were after," Gray concluded.

The story was already so jumbled that I didn't need this new observation, but it had the saving grace of being correct. I reminded myself to make sure I compared notes with Gray on future cases.

"Gray, I had not thought of that," I told him.

"It's just crazy enough to make sense."

"So there they were, the Springers double-crossing Dennis, Sally and her buddies double-crossing both Dennis and the Springers, and the cops jumping the gun. Spears and the other detectives set off Baxter's car alarm to get him to come out and give them an excuse to search the car, but it sounds like he didn't give them the provocation they wanted and they began doubting themselves.

"So they called the D.A., who went nuts and told them to impound the car and wait until he got there. That was about the time that the kid from the desk was letting them into Baxter's room, and so Spears pulled them out of there and put a guard on the door. It was just enough time for the kid to see Baxter's Rolex, and then Canfield, the manager, got there. The kid went around back, crawled through the window, stole the watch, and then went shopping through Baxter's things."

"Bet he was surprised at what he found," Gray said.

"Oh, yeah. So when the news stories never mentioned the money, Sally and her friends figured Dennis had somehow managed to get it. That's why they were so interested in his cab ride that night, and if he was carrying anything."

"So that's why she didn't ask him about the money before she killed him. She didn't know it was missing."

"Actually, she told me why she did it, before the bail guys came through the door. The way she saw it, Dennis abandoned her, and probably to die, too. She said he betrayed her. That is one little girl you don't want to disappoint."

"So you think she and her buddies had parted company when they learned he was dead?"

"Not sure. She gave them that photo booth picture so they could go pull their bail bonds act on the motel clerk and then on me, so they were still together the next day. And somebody gave her a lift out to Exile the night she visited me, so I think they probably didn't have their falling out until later."

"You suppose she meant to double-cross them all along?" Gray asked.

"Yes, I do. She had that gun for a reason, even before she decided to kill Dennis, and she kept it for a reason, too. Believe me, when Ames and Knight came through that door at the Seaview they were under no illusions about the partnership."

"So what was the story with that stolen credit card?"

"More lying. Dennis never intended to sign in at the motel. He bribed Billy Lee later that night with two twenty-dollar bills, and he did the same thing with the guy at the desk. Apparently the clerk had a habit of renting rooms at a discount and pocketing the money without ever creating a record of the rental. He could get away with it because Canfield, the manager, was almost never there at night."

"Too busy cheating on his wife."

"Exactly. When the police showed up and Dennis ran off, the kid got a little concerned that someone might have seen Dennis there and that the police might go over the night's guest list. So he pulled out an old credit card that had been sitting in their Lost and Found drawer for over a year, made an imprint, and concocted the story about the credit checker being down."

Gray nodded. "Because running that card through would have shown it was expired a year before, and probably canceled before that."

"Right again. It was a hoax, but the funny part about

it is that the Sharps' lawyer came up with a similar story to explain why they knew where Dennis was that night. They said he was a normal runaway, and that he had just used a family credit card that they were watching closely."

"So why didn't your friend Winslow get a copy of the receipt and see it wasn't the same name, or that it was expired?"

"He thought he was working a straight runaway case. When he walked in and asked about Dennis, the clerk was only too happy to say he'd seen him run out the door the prior evening and that it was a Midnight cab that took him away. The subject of the receipt never came up, and Winslow headed off to the Midnight stand thinking he was hot on the trail of a kid running away from home."

Gray looked at the chessboard, and was starting to set the pieces up again for a real game when a car horn sounded nearby. It was a little after eight on a bright, sunny day at the beach, and a Midnight Taxi Service van was pulling up.

A large fat man hoisted himself from the front seat and began lumbering toward us. It was Ruby, and although it was already eighty degrees, he still wore the hat and the windbreaker.

"Hey, where's the coffee?" I called out.

"Oh, that darn nephew of Corelli's got that all horsed up this morning. He's never gonna work out."

He laughed as he approached, and stuck his hand out to Gray.

"Hi. Ruby Sears. I used to work with the Yankee here."

"Gray Toliver. Used to be a Yankee myself, about a hundred years ago, but I converted when I married a Southerner."

"Best way to keep peace in a marriage. Surrender right at the beginning." Ruby looked at the table, and then at me. "You ready?"

"For what?" I asked.

"Your buddy is comin' in from New York in an hour, isn't he? Wanted to ride in a Midnight cab?"

"Well, he wanted me to drive him, actually."

"I know. That's why I brought the van, so I wouldn't be tempted to let you take the wheel." He turned to Gray. "Yankee, huh? You know, Frank thinks he didn't fit in with us because he's from up north, and graduated from college and all. But that ain't it.

"His name's the problem. Frank Cole. Doesn't end in an 'e' sound. Sticks out like a sore thumb. Manny, Tony, Billy Lee, Danny, Ruby, and Frank. See?"

"Corelli's first name is Dominic," I protested.

"And we all call him Corelli, with an 'e' sound. So what do you say we go get this friend of yours?"

"Is this the famous Mark Ruben I've heard so much about? Architect of the starve-yourself-to-show-you-mean-business strategy?" Gray had never been a fan of Mark's plan to wait out my persecutors.

"That's him, and it's starting to look like the delaying tactics aren't working." I brightened. "But I did make a fair amount of change on this last case, so at least I can afford a good meal from time to time."

"Paid by two convicted felons. Weren't you supposed to keep your nose clean down here?" Gray never forgot a thing anyone ever said to him, which was one of the annoying ways in which he reminded me of my ex-wife.

"Hey, I was paid by Winslow's firm. All free and legal—"

"You comin' or not—" Ruby asked, before adding with a mischievous grin "—Frankie?"

* * * * *

REQUEST YOUR FREE BOOKS!

2 FREE NOVELS
PLUS 2 FREE GIFTS!

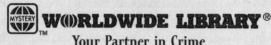

WORLDWIDE LIBRARY®

Your Partner in Crime

YES! Please send me 2 FREE novels from the Worldwide Library® series and my 2 FREE gifts (gifts are worth about $10). After receiving them, if I don't wish to receive any more books, I can return the shipping statement marked "cancel." If I don't cancel, I will receive 4 brand-new novels every month and be billed just $5.24 per book in the U.S. or $6.24 per book in Canada. That's a saving of at least 34% off the cover price. It's quite a bargain! Shipping and handling is just 50¢ per book in the U.S. and 75¢ per book in Canada.* I understand that accepting the 2 free books and gifts places me under no obligation to buy anything. I can always return a shipment and cancel at any time. Even if I never buy another book, the two free books and gifts are mine to keep forever.

414/424 WDN FEJ3

Name _____ (PLEASE PRINT) _____

Address _____ Apt. #

City _____ State/Prov. _____ Zip/Postal Code

Signature (if under 18, a parent or guardian must sign)

Mail to the **Reader Service:**
IN U.S.A.: P.O. Box 1867, Buffalo, NY 14240-1867
IN CANADA: P.O. Box 609, Fort Erie, Ontario L2A 5X3

Not valid for current subscribers to the Worldwide Library series.

Want to try two free books from another line?
Call 1-800-873-8635 or visit www.ReaderService.com.

* Terms and prices subject to change without notice. Prices do not include applicable taxes. Sales tax applicable in N.Y. Canadian residents will be charged applicable taxes. Offer not valid in Quebec. This offer is limited to one order per household. All orders subject to credit approval. Credit or debit balances in a customer's account(s) may be offset by any other outstanding balance owed by or to the customer. Please allow 4 to 6 weeks for delivery. Offer available while quantities last.

Your Privacy—The Reader Service is committed to protecting your privacy. Our Privacy Policy is available online at www.ReaderService.com or upon request from the Reader Service.

We make a portion of our mailing list available to reputable third parties that offer products we believe may interest you. If you prefer that we not exchange your name with third parties, or if you wish to clarify or modify your communication preferences, please visit us at www.ReaderService.com/consumerschoice or write to us at Reader Service Preference Service, P.O. Box 9062, Buffalo, NY 14269. Include your complete name and address.

WWLI1B

"Search," Cha[...]

The golden retriever sh[...]
house. Keeping a hand on [...]
close as the K-9 entered a roo[...] end of the
A nursery. Chase's stomach clenc[...] stayed
[...] of the hall.

Zoe Jenkins lay crumpled on the floor b[...]
of ceiling that had fallen. Chase could hea[...] chunk
crying.

His heart contracted in his chest. Was the woma[...]
dead? Swiftly he pushed aside the plaster. "Ma'am?"

She didn't move. The baby continued to cry, its pitiful
wails muffled by the mother, whose dark brown hair
shielded her face. Dash whined as if he, too, were
worried.

With his heart in his throat, Chase knelt, hoping to find
a pulse...

* * *

Mountain Country K-9 Unit

Books by Terri Reed

Love Inspired Suspense

Buried Mountain Secrets
Secret Mountain Hideout
Christmas Protection Detail
Secret Sabotage
Forced to Flee
Forced to Hide
Undercover Christmas Escape
Shielding the Innocent Target

Rocky Mountain K-9 Unit

Detection Detail

Pacific Northwest K-9 Unit

Explosive Trail

Mountain Country K-9 Unit

Search and Detect

Visit the Author Profile page at LoveInspired.com for more titles.